ROOM TO SWING

ED LACY

Edited, with an introduction and notes,
by Leslie S. Klinger

Published by Poisoned Pen Press, an imprint of Sourcebooks,
in association with the Library of Congress
P.O. Box 4410, Naperville, Illinois 60567-4410
(630) 961-3900
sourcebooks.com

This edition of *Room to Swing* is based on the first edition in the Library of
Congress's collection, originally published in 1957 by Harper & Brothers.

Cataloging-in-Publication Data is on file with the Library of Congress.

Printed and bound in the United States of America.
VP 10 9 8 7 6 5 4 3 2 1

CONTENTS

FOREWORD

Crime writing as we know it first appeared in 1841, with the publication of "The Murders in the Rue Morgue." Written by American author Edgar Allan Poe, the short story introduced C. Auguste Dupin, the world's first wholly fictional detective. Other American and British authors had begun working in the genre by the 1860s, and by the 1920s we had officially entered the golden age of detective fiction.

Throughout this short history, many authors who paved the way have been lost or forgotten. Library of Congress Crime Classics bring back into print some of the finest American crime writing from the 1860s to the 1960s, showcasing rare and lesser-known titles that represent a range of genres, from cozies to police procedurals. With cover designs inspired by images from the Library's collections, each book in this series includes the original text, reproduced faithfully from an early edition in the Library's collections and complete with strange spellings and unorthodox punctuation. Also included are a contextual introduction, a brief biography of the author, notes, recommendations for further reading, and suggested discussion questions. Our hope is for these books to start conversations, inspire further research, and bring obscure works to a new generation of readers.

Early American crime fiction is not only entertaining to read, but it also sheds light on the culture of its time. While many of the titles in this series include outmoded language and stereotypes now considered offensive, these books give readers the opportunity to reflect on how our society's perceptions of race, gender, ethnicity, and social standing have evolved over more than a century.

More dark secrets and bloody deeds lurk in the massive collections of the Library of Congress. I encourage you to explore these works for yourself, here in Washington, DC, or online at www.loc.gov.

—Carla D. Hayden, Librarian of Congress

INTRODUCTION

By the time Ed Lacy's *Room to Swing* was published in 1957, a small but growing number of Black sleuths were featured in the world of American crime writing.* In 1900, Pauline Hopkins, the Black editor of *Colored American Magazine*, published several crime fiction short stories. A few years later, her novel *Hagar's Daughter: A Story of Southern Caste Prejudice* appeared, which has many elements of crime fiction, including amateur detecting by Venus Johnson, a young Black maid. *The Black Sleuth*, though incomplete, was written and published by Black author John Edward Bruce between 1907 and 1908 and featured a Black private detective. In the 1920s, White author Octavus Roy Cohen created Florian Slappey, a caricature of a Black detective who appeared nearly weekly in the *Saturday Evening Post*. The brilliant Harlem Renaissance writer Rudolph Fisher published *The Conjure-Man Dies* in 1932, featuring a Black police detective and a Black amateur detective, with a story

---

* In 1820, Black Congregational minister and Revolutionary War hero Lemuel Haynes published *Mystery Developed*, the first true crime narrative by a Black writer.

set entirely in Harlem.* In 1933, two short stories by Chester Himes appeared featuring the Black police detectives Coffin Ed Johnson and Grave Digger Jones, prefiguring Himes's Harlem Cycle detective series that debuted in 1958.

By midcentury, Black characters were well established in the ranks of official detectives. Hughes Allison was the first Black writer to have a story appear in *Ellery Queen Mystery Magazine,* with his 1948 tale, "Corollary," featuring Detective Joe Hill. Queen himself introduced Detective Zilgitt, a Black police officer, in *Cat of Many Tails* (1949), and Officer Connolly is a character in Bar Spicer's *Blues for the Prince* (1950). A Black manservant, Webster Flagg, is an amateur sleuth in two novels by Veronica Parker Johns, *Murder by the Day* (1953) and *Servant's Problem* (1958).

Though private investigators were the most popular figures in crime writing, especially in the work of Dashiell Hammett, Raymond Chandler, Ellery Queen, and Rex Stout, no one had created a Black hard-boiled private eye in a noir setting until Ed Lacy's *Room to Swing*. Noir (from the French, meaning "black") was an attitude or point of view that pervaded film and crime fiction in the 1940s and 1950s. Cynical, morally ambiguous protagonists often found themselves caught in a whirlpool of events, slowly sucked into disaster.† For the compassionate observer, there were clear parallels with the daily lives of Black men and women of the era, who treaded cautiously through White America. Lacy's lead was followed (and somewhat overshadowed) by Himes's books, mentioned above, and Ernest Tidyman's 1970 novel *Shaft,*

---

* *The Conjure-Man Dies* was republished as part of the Library of Congress Crime Classics series in 2022.

---

† Perhaps the greatest filmic exposition of this maelstrom is the 1947 *Out of the Past,* with Robert Mitchum, Kirk Douglas, and Jane Greer, directed by Jacque Tourneur.

which featured a two-fisted Harlem private eye (and spawned a series of films).*

Lacy (the pseudonym of Leonard S. Zinberg) was White, but he was married to a Black woman and lived for many years in Harlem, where he enjoyed a more integrated social life than was typical of that time. Although Lacy was not writing from a place of lived experience, he made an earnest effort to capture the unique struggles of a Black man in the 1950s. Scholar Frankie Y. Bailey, in her groundbreaking *Out of the Woodpile: Black Characters in Crime and Detective Fiction*, notes with approval that Marcia Muller (honored in 2005 by the Mystery Writers of America as a grand master) calls Lacy's protagonist "the first convincing [B]lack detective in crime fiction."†

Whether Lacy achieved that distinction or not, his central character is a great addition to the tradition of the hard-boiled detective. Toussaint Garvey Moore is a man of contradictions. His name links him to Black nationalist causes, but Touie is apolitical. "He is literate, intelligent, ethical, physically powerful, and sensitive, often to a greater degree than his

---

* Others in the Black "tough guy" genre include the Chicago-based Big Bull Benson, the creation of Black writer Percy Spurlark Parker, who features in a series of short stories and the novels *Good Girls Don't Get Murdered* (1973) and *An Unrefusable Request* (2009; a bibliography of the Benson tales is at https://thrillingdetective .com/2021/02/04/big-bull-benson). Carver Bascombe, a San Francisco PI created by Kenn Davis, appears in eight novels beginning in 1976 with *The Dark Side* (the first was coauthored with John Stanley). Another long-lived creation is Robert Parker's Hawk, the Black mercenary who is the sidekick of the exceedingly popular Boston-based investigator Spenser. Hawk debuts in *Promised Land* (1976) and appears in virtually all of the thirty-six subsequent Spenser novels, as well as the nine Spenser novels penned by Parker's literary heir, Ace Atkins.

---

† Frankie Y. Bailey, *Out of the Woodpile: Black Characters in Crime and Detective Fiction* (New York: Greenwood Press, 1991), 81. Muller's comment is found in *1001 Midnights: The Aficionado's Guide to Mystery and Detective Fiction*, edited by Muller and Bill Pronzini (New York: Arbor House, 1986), 456–57.

[W]hite counterparts," remarks Vicki K. Robinson in her essay in *Critical Survey of Mystery and Detective Fiction.** His race puts him squarely in the middle of trouble. Hired for a surveillance job because he is Black, Moore soon finds himself framed for the murder of a White man. To clear his name, Moore must travel to southern Ohio, where he hides out in a tiny Black community until he finds the information he needs. Moore then returns to New York to trap the killer and confront his White accusers.

Lacy wisely presents the story without stereotyping and without the dogmatic self-righteousness found in later works depicting confrontations between Blacks and Whites. Moore is quick to assert himself as a Black man, but he also resents White liberals who patronize him. There are no polemics about the unfairness of race relations, no burning quest for justice. He values his work for the independence it provides, even if he makes very little at it. At the beginning of the case, Moore is excited that he has the opportunity to start his own detective agency. His girlfriend urges him to give up his infatuation with private eyes and take a real job at the post office. In the end, Moore comes around to her point of view. In his own words:

> *I'm sick of phonies. I want to be a mailman and mind my own business. Let somebody else be waiting to collar a babe shoplifting because she hasn't money to buy the clothes she needs. I don't ever want to dun an old woman into paying up on some goddamned sink on which she was screwed from the word go. Most of all I'm sick of being around people busy stepping on each other's backs, turning in their own relatives for a job, murdering them to keep a job... In short, I'm sick to death of playing in other people's dirt.*†

---

* Vicki K. Robinson, "Ed Lacy/Leonard S. Zinberg," *Critical Survey of Mystery and Detective Fiction*, vol. 3, Frank N. Magill, ed. (Pasadena, CA: Salem Press, 1988), 1018.

---

† Page 184.

Lacy uses as an epigraph a quotation from Thomas Jefferson: "The mass of mankind has not been born with saddles on their backs, nor a favored few booted and spurred." This famous statement is from what was then thought to be Jefferson's last letter, dated June 24, 1826.* The letter was written in response to an invitation to participate in a celebration of the fiftieth anniversary of the Declaration of Independence. Was Lacy aware of the irony that Jefferson owned slaves and did not mean these words to apply to Black residents of the United States?

Perhaps true to the 1950s, Moore is a little slow to understand the nature of the relationship between his employer, Kay, and her partner, Barbara (whom she calls "Butch"). However, ultimately, Moore treats the gay couple sympathetically (although he regards Kay as one of those "phonies" that he disdains). By the time of the events in the sequel to Room to Swing, he is willing enough to accept additional employment from her and asks politely after Barbara, though it's clear that he and his wife have not been so open-minded as to actually socialize with the couple.

The book is no sociological tract. The mystery in Room to Swing is well plotted, based in the characters' pasts; the writing is stylistically interesting as a series of flashbacks; and Touie Moore is a vibrant, compelling character.

Although Room to Swing won the Edgar Award from the Mystery Writers of America for Best Novel, at least one pair of critics thought it not even the best of Lacy's work.† That honor, they asserted, should go to Lacy's only other story about

---

* In 2004, two later letters were discovered. The June 24 letter, and most of Jefferson's papers, are held by the Library of Congress. Thomas Jefferson to Roger C. Weightman, June 24, 1826, http://hdl.loc.gov/loc.mss/mtj.mtjbib024904. Thomas Jefferson Papers, http://hdl.loc.gov/loc.mss/collmss.ms000014.

† Robert A. Baker and Michael T. Nietzel, Private Eyes: One Hundred and One Knights, A Survey of American Detective Fiction, 1922–1984 (Bowling Green, OH: Bowling Green State University Popular Press, 1985), 101.

Moore, a sequel called *Moment of Untruth*. Moore has given up investigative work for that job at the post office. When he learns that his wife is pregnant, he is afraid that the loss of her income will make their modest lifestyle unaffordable, and he takes on another detective job to earn some extra money. His response to the announcement of her pregnancy is telling (though he keeps it to himself): "Damn, just what the world needed—one more kid…another colored kid!"*

Room to Swing is a remarkable achievement for more than its status as a milestone in the history of Black crime fiction. It is noteworthy for its honest and insightful depiction of Black lives in 1950s America, many elements of which are still familiar today. And it's a clever and suspenseful mystery, one of the standouts among the enormous quantity of noir crime fiction produced in the mid-twentieth century, by a forgotten master. All this adds up to a book well worth reading!

—Leslie S. Klinger

---

* Ed Lacy, *Moment of Untruth* (New York: Lancer Books, 1964), 7.

"The mass of mankind has not been born with saddles on their backs, nor a favored few booted and spurred."

—Thomas Jefferson

NOW

1

I broke par* in Bingston.† It's a little town of a couple of thousand in southern Ohio and you can take in the entire town in
about three minutes. It took me less than a minute to learn all I
wanted to know—that I'd made a mistake coming here.

The main drag looks bigger than it should because they get
a lot of trade from nearby farms. I parked my car in front of the
largest store—a drugstore—and went in. The few people passing stared at me like I'd stepped out of a flying saucer. Okay,
even though my Jaguar is an eight-year-old job I picked up for
six hundred bucks, any foreign heap attracts attention.‡ A fact

---

* "Broke par" is a golfing expression, meaning beating the average (par) score.

---

† There is no "Bingston" in Ohio, but Kingston is a virtually all-White village in southern Ohio of just more than a thousand residents (as of the 1960 census). The village is
reported as far back as 1805.

---

‡ Foreign cars were still quite rare in the United States in 1957. An eight-year-old Jaguar
would either be a model XK120 roadster, a topless curvaceous two-seater, or a large
four-door saloon, model MK IV. It seems most likely that this was the roadster, which
was "low-slung" (as Touie later describes it) and the fastest production car made in
1949. However, it was an open vehicle (no top); models with a fixed top or "drop-head"
(convertible) top were not marketed until 1951 and 1953, respectively—too late to be
an "eight-year-old job" in 1957. This is probably a mistake by Lacy; if this were an open
model, one would have expected Frances, who complained about the cold before going
with Touie in his car, to have worn something warm or at least a headscarf for a drive in
an open car.

which was worrying me nuts at the moment; attention was the last thing I needed.

I was a positive sensation inside the store—everything stopped dead still. The fat soda jerk stared at me with disbelief, a guy having breakfast at the counter spun around, toast in mouth, and made big eyes, the druggist was getting some mail from an old Negro postman and they both looked startled. It was a well-stocked place, more like a general store. I saw the phone booths and walked over. The Bingston phone book is about the size and thickness of a Broadway theater program. There wasn't any May Russell listed.

Figuring there had to be more to the phone book than this booklet, I started toward the soda jerk to ask. He reacted like a ham actor, his round face showing horror, then a fat grin of relief as he glanced at the door. I turned to see a cop coming at me, coming fast. Some small-town cops sport musical-comedy uniforms. This one was a stocky, middle-aged joker in high-polished black boots, gray breeches with a wide purple stripe down the sides, leather windbreaker with the largest badge I ever saw, and a kind of cowboy hat. There wasn't any doubt as to why he was coming; his gun was loose in its holster and he was actually holding a billy in his right hand. I didn't see how they could be looking for me so soon, but my stomach began turning somersaults. I got set; if I could flatten this cop and make the door I was safe.

The mailman was suddenly in my way, both hands on my right fist as he whispered, "Relax, son."

"Get out of my face!" I said, pulling my hand away. The cop was on top of us. The mailman nodded at him and said, "Hello, Mr. Williams."

"Hello, Sam. Anything for me?"

"I left a few letters at your office," the postman said, still blocking me.

The cop asked me, "Stranger in town, *boy?*"

"Yeah." I'd been called *boy* more times in the last half a dozen hours than in my whole life.

"That's what I thought. I'd better explain a few things to you."

"What things?" I said, my eyes on his billy hand. I pushed the mailman out of the way but the damn fool stepped right back in front of me.

"What you doing here, boy?"

"Looking in the phone book. That against the law?"

"Nope. I thought maybe you was thinking of eating in here. Being new, maybe you don't know it ain't the custom for colored to eat in here."

I got a little mad and I relaxed, almost sagged with relief. I was still in the clear. The crazy thing that stuck in my mind was that this cop had a kind face, and, if anything, he was talking very *gently*—with the billy ready for action. I told him, "I wasn't planning on eating the phone book."

The cop grinned, his eyes taking in my Fifth Avenue clothes—and he'd sure seen the Jaguar outside. Then his eyes went over my broken nose and the fact I had about a half a foot and at least sixty pounds on him, and he looked a trifle unhappy again. "Understand, I don't want no trouble. Being you're a new boy around here, I want to straighten you out."

"Then we're straight. That all there is to the phone book?" I nodded toward the booths.

"That's the phone book. Who you looking for?"

"Must have the wrong town. I didn't see the party listed," I said, walking around the mailman, heading for the door.

The postman said, "I know about everybody in Bingston," and his brown face said plainly, "As one Negro to another, let me help you."

"That's okay, forget it." I walked outside and looked up and down the main street, saw it all without straining my neck. A movie, two small hotels, several supermarkets, a couple dozen stores, and maybe another "business" street crossing this one about a block down.

As somebody once said, there are more horses' asses than horses in the world, and at the moment I felt like the number-one rear. I'd been crazy driving fifteen hours to this hayseed town where I stuck out like a sore thumb. Still, I was here, and maybe the answer was, too.

The Tom* letter carrier was standing beside me. He said, "Guess you must be from up North. Bingston isn't a mean town for colored, just a little old-fashioned. No sense getting into trouble, son."

"Skip the race-relations lecture, Uncle. You know a May Russell?"

A darker anger flooded his brown face at "Uncle." He started to walk away, saw the cop watching us from the store door. He turned back and told me, "Look, we don't want trouble in this town. I've lived here all my life and our people have made progress in Bingston."

"You going to straighten me out, too? I stop to look at a phone booth and I'm trouble. How far south is Ohio?"

"Asking for May Russell will start real trouble. She isn't for colored men."

"What's that mean?"

"She's a...a...scarlet lady!" he whispered.

I broke down and laughed. I hadn't heard that phrase since I

---

* Touie refers to Mr. Davis as an "Uncle Tom," a Black man acting in a subservient manner to get along in White society (derived from the lead character in Harriet Beecher Stowe's novel *Uncle Tom's Cabin* [1852], who was viewed by many readers as inappropriately kind to White slaveholders).

read *The Scarlet Letter** in high school lit and was disappointed that it wasn't hot stuff. The mailman laughed a little, showing crooked teeth. "Got me wrong, Pops. There a hotel where I can put up for a couple of days?"

"No hotel here, for colored. We only have thirty-nine Negro families in Bingston."

"Hell, doesn't Ohio have a civil-rights law, or any—?"

"We're right on the border of Kentucky, so—" He waved a stubby brown hand southward. "We don't get many out-of-town colored persons. Mrs. Kelly takes in roomers but she's full up. How long do you plan on staying?"

"Couple days. I'm a...a musician. I'm on my way up to Chicago; thought this May Russell was the friend of a guy I knew."

"I knew you were theater folk. What's the name of this friend you're looking for? Knowing everybody here is my business."

"An army buddy. Just called him Joe....Must have the wrong town," I said, lying wildly. "Tell you the truth, Pops, I've been on the road a lot and have a slight cold. I want to rest up for a few days."

"You certainly don't look sick. I'm Sam Davis. I suppose I can put you up at my house."

"Thanks. I'm Harry Jones," I said, picking a clever name out of the air.

As we shook hands he said, "Will two dollars a night† and a dollar for meals be all right?"

"Perfect."

---

* The famous 1850 novel by Nathaniel Hawthorne, in which an adulteress is required to wear a letter "A" emblazoned on her bodice to shame her. Although Hester Prynne, the wearer of the scarlet letter, is called a "scarlet woman," the phrase derives from the vision described in Revelation 17 of "the Mother of Harlots," who is dressed in purple and scarlet.

---

† This would be the equivalent of $18.40 per night in 2021. Samuel H. Williamson, "Seven Ways to Compute the Relative Value of a U. S. Dollar, 1790 to Present," Measuring Worth, 2021, https://www.measuringworth.com/. Even the Motel 6 in Kingston, Ohio, charges more than four times that amount in 2021!

"I'll phone Mary, my wife, that you're coming. You turn left on Elm, at the traffic light down the street. Then you keep walking for about five blocks and you'll see a brick house with wooden ducks on the front lawn. Wire fence. That's mine. You'll be in the colored section. Ask anybody for Sam Davis' house. Not too much of a walk."

"I'm on rubber," I said, nodding at the Jaguar. He was impressed, asked, "Can you do a hundred in that?"

"With the gas pedal off the floor. Thanks for the room. I'll go right out and grab some sleep. Think it would cause a riot if I buy the local paper first?"

"Now, now, Mr. Jones, Bingston isn't that bad. The *News* don't come out till noon, unless you want yesterday's copy."

"Yesterday's will do. Like to read myself asleep."

"You can buy one at the Smoke Shop across the street. I'll phone Mary that you're coming out."

I got the paper and, as I slid behind the wheel, the cop walked over and asked, chummy-like, "This a European auto?"

He was really friendly, yet if I wanted to get a cup of coffee in the drugstore he would bash my head in. "English."

"Pretty expensive, I bet?"

"You win the bet," I said, starting the Jag.

"Any better than our cars?"

"No," I said, backing out. I made the turn at the traffic light and pulled over to the curb. Elm Street was a lot of big houses with even bigger lawns. The paper had used the wire story from New York about a Richard Tutt being found beaten to death in his room, and that the police were looking for "a" Negro. Fingerprints had revealed Tutt's real name to be Robert Thomas and that he was a wanted criminal. At the bottom there were a few puff paragraphs about Thomas having been born in Bingston and wanted by the local police for the last six years.

There wasn't anything I didn't know already, so I put the paper down and drove on.

The postman's house was better than I expected: old, but solidly built. In fact most of the houses in this "Negro" section looked pretty good. There was a driveway and a garage in the back. I parked in the driveway, in the rear of the house, locked the car. My license plates were muddy enough.* A plump woman with a warm brown face opened the door, said, "You must be Mr. Jones. Come in. I've hardly had time to straighten up the guest room. Haven't used it since my cousin Allen, from Dayton, was here. Take me a minute to dust and—"

"I'm pooped," I said, suddenly aching with tiredness. "I'd like to go to bed now."

"You must think I'm a terrible housekeeper."

"I don't. I'm too tired to think anything. Can I go to my room now?"

"As you wish. You do look tired. I'll get you a towel. Where are your bags?"

"In the car," I lied. "I'll get them later."

I followed her upstairs to a large room filled with old, heavy furniture. The bed looked wonderful. She gave me a towel, said the bathroom was down the hall, and kept chattering about the dust and things. The room looked neat as a pin to me. I stopped her mouth by hanging my Harris-tweed overcoat in the large closet. She stood in the doorway, said, "Mr. Davis told you two dollars a night and—"

"Yeah." I gave her a five-dollar bill.

"Well, he was wrong about the meals. Food's gone up. It will be two dollars a day instead of one for meals."

"Okay."

---

* That is, it would take an effort to read the numbers and trace the car.

"I'll give you your change later." She hesitated, pulled at her apron with the money hand. "I hope you're not a drinking man, Mr. Jones."

"I'm only a tired man. Good day, Mrs. Davis." When she left I hung up my coat, locked the door, hid my wallet and badge under the mattress, the data on Thomas under the rug. Taking off my nylon shirt and underwear, I made sure the hallway was empty and sprinted to the bathroom. It was the largest can I'd ever seen. I took a fast shower, washing my shirt and stuff, toweled myself dry, and made another nude sprint down the hallway. I hung up the shirt and underwear carefully, pulled the shades down, and jumped into bed.

I wanted to think; I *had* to think if I wanted to get out of this mess. But I hadn't slept in two days and the bed was soft as a good dream. When I jerked myself awake the pale green hands on my wrist watch said it was ten o'clock. I'd pounded my ear for a dozen hours. I felt great—and mad as hell at wasting all that time.

I pulled up the shades; it was very dark outside, the dim street lights blocks apart. My wash was dry and I got my pipe working as I dressed. It wouldn't be safe to hang around this burg for more than a day or two, if it was safe at all. Normally it would be a cinch to shake a little town like Bingston clean in two days, only it was south and I had dark skin. I'd stand out and somebody would peg me as "the" Negro being hunted by the New York police.

I was too much of a stranger. If I only had a contact, somebody in town to do the more obvious asking around. Old super sleuth me, what asking? I didn't have idea one as to what I was looking for. A hick town could be either a wonderful hideout or a trap.

Taking out the TV data on Bob Thomas I read through it for the tenth time. I felt a little better, still had a hunch the killer had to come from Bingston. Unless it was a freak job, one that didn't fit any pattern. If it was a crazy killing, then I might as well go back and put it down in the electric chair.

The house was so quiet I knew the old couple were asleep. And I was hungry enough to see what the refrigerator held. The TV was on, giving the parlor an unreal glow. There was a young girl watching the screen. I could see her face clearly, a lean dark face, skin as dark as mine, hair piled atop her head *au naturel.* When she saw me she stood up and turned on a lamp. She was wearing a simple knitted gray suit that clung to her tall, strong figure. In the light she looked older than I thought, about twenty-seven. Her nose was short, her eyes large and deep, and she had full, heavy lips.

"Mr. Jones? I'm Frances Davis. Mom said you might want supper. Do you?"

The voice was low and sullen, maybe even bitter. "Where is everybody?"

"Asleep. It's after ten—late for us."

"Sorry I kept you up. I'll go out and grab a bite."

"Where? There aren't any 'colored' restaurants here. You didn't keep me up; I'm a TV bug. If you want to eat follow me into the kitchen."

"Doesn't seem much worth getting up for at any time in Bingston," I said as she walked by me toward the kitchen. She was about six feet tall, and in flat shoes.

"Not if your skin isn't pale." She stopped in front of me. "Your shoulders make you seem short. You're not. And your clothes— they're the end. You're really togged down."*

Up close her face looked a little on the cute side, the heavy lips and eyes interesting. "Thanks, honey. I like your suit too."

* Hipster and Black slang (what Touie calls "jive talk") for "dressed in style."

"Bought it in Cincinnati last year. How did you break your nose?" she asked, opening the kitchen door.

"Played football a lot of years ago. Had a pigskin scholarship— till the war came." The kitchen was big and bright, and a little crazy: very modern refrigerator and freezer, electric washing machine and electric grill—and an old-fashioned coal-burning stove polished a glistening black. She pointed toward a white table and I sat down as she took various pots out of the refrigerator, which was stocked with food. "Greens, rice, roast pork, biscuits, potatoes, and pie. Coffee or tea. Okay?"

"Fine, but I'll skip the biscuits and potatoes. And tea."

"What's your instrument and what band are you with?"

"Drums. I'm not with any outfit at the moment. Been playing a few club dates down in New Orleans and Lake Charles— heading up to Chicago for some more. Mostly wildcat jobs."

"How's New Orleans?"

"Hot and damp. I was glad to blow the city."

"Man, I dug your Jaguar outside. It's the greatest."

"Honey, why don't you cut the phony jive talk?"

She turned from the coal stove, which must have been going all the time—the kitchen was overwarm. "I was putting it on for you, being you are a jazz man. Speaking of phony things, stop calling me honey."

"Okay, Miss Frances. And I didn't mean to talk out of turn."

She gave me a quiet stare as she started loading my plate. "I took it as a compliment, Mr. Jones. Tell me, why did you come to Bingston?"

I didn't get the compliment angle. And it was time I started asking questions. Between mouthfuls of the fine food I said, "No reason, merely passing through and thought I'd rest up for a couple of days. I was reading the Bingston paper this morning; seems like you had a little excitement here—a local lad was killed in New York. Did you know this Tutt—or Thomas?"

"I remember him but I didn't know him. He was white. I read about his being killed. You know, the older I get the more I'm convinced whites are crazy."

I nodded, swallowed a lot of rice. "You remind me of my old man. He was a nationalist.* Last thing I expected to find...here."

"You mean in this wide-spot-in-the-road," she said, sitting opposite me, nibbling on a small hunk of pie. Her brown skin looked velvet smooth, and the kitchen light showed rather high cheekbones. "We didn't have to fight for integration here—this isn't really 'South.' Yet Bingston is a prison with color bars. A Negro girl can only work at certain jobs; she has a choice, or a chance, of marrying only two or three single men; must live within a certain area; can't eat anyplace but—but you know that too."

"A small town is a small town, even for whites."

"And ten times as small for us!"

"Must be buses leaving here every day. This Thomas guy took off, and look how he ended up. What does Bingston think of his murder? Any—eh—fuss because a Negro was supposed to have done it?"

"It was different for him here; he was white, although a poor one. They even were doing a TV show about him. Sometimes I think of trying to make it in New York or Los Angeles—but I'm scared. You can be lonely in a big city too. Be different if I knew people there. And I've seen pictures of the Harlem and South Side slums, know they aren't any paradise."

"True, but at least you have more room to swing. Maybe this Thomas swung too wide?"

She shrugged her shoulders, seemed to have larger breasts than

---

* That is, an advocate of a Black nation to which Black Americans would migrate.

I'd thought. "I dream a lot about leaving here. Sometimes Bingston seems a living cemetery for me. Then I tell myself I'm living in a comfortable house with my folks, why should I run away? This is my town as much as the ofays"—why give it to them?"

"Doesn't Ohio have a civil-rights law?" I asked over another forkful of rice and gravy. Her words were giving me an idea—if I worked it right maybe I'd found my local helper.

"You mean do we fight back? Sure. As I told you, it isn't the actual law here as much as custom. But in the long run they mean the same thing. We're only a handful and most of us have 'good' jobs. For instance, I could make and save a lot of money as a domestic. But a few of us try to raise some sand†—we've just won a two-year fight to sit in the orchestra of the movie house instead of the balcony. Big deal." She shook her head. "I shouldn't say that; it *was* a big thing. Only—damn, there has to be more to living than sitting in the orchestra."

"What do you do? Going to college?"

"My brother is at Howard. It makes me burn, Pop insisting on sending him to a colored college. I wanted him to go to Ohio State. Another lost battle. I couldn't go to college. It wasn't a question of money—I'm just a female and marriage should be my career. Bunk!"

"Your folks are old-fashioned."

"Pop finally sent me to a business school up in Dayton, as if anybody needs a brown secretary in Bingston. I work as a

---

* The great Harlem Renaissance author Rudolph Fisher, author of *The Conjure-Man Dies* (1932), in an appendix to his 1928 novel, *The Walls of Jericho* (Ann Arbor: University of Michigan Press, 1984), offered "An Introduction to Contemporary Harlemese, Expurgated and Abridged" (hereinafter, *Harlemese*). In that "dictionary," Fisher defined "ofay" as "a person who, so far as is known, is white. Fay is said to be the original term, and ofay a contraction of 'old' and 'fay'" (299).

---

† According to Tom Dalzell and Terry Victor, eds., *The New Partridge Dictionary of Slang and Unconventional English* (London: Routledge, 2006; hereinafter, *Partridge*), "to argue loudly, creating a problem" (1854).

part-time typist for Mr. Ross, a mealy-mouthed tan lawyer and real-estate hustler. Has a family and a hobby—trying to make me. I also have a part-time job in a bakery a few blocks from here—result of another battle. That's what kills me; we have to *fight* for a lousy job selling cakes. Want your tea now?"

"Yes, thanks." I cut into the pie. It was wonderful. "Has this Thomas killing started any feeling here against colored?"

"No. If anything, people are relieved that he's dead."

"According to the papers he was a one-man crime wave before he took off."

"He jumped bail."

"He was in for rape and assault, wasn't he?"

She got up to get the tea. For no reason I noticed her legs were strong and not skinny. I sugared the tea as she sat down again, took out a pack of butts. I pointed to my pipe sticking out of my breast pocket as I got a match working. She blew a small cloud of smoke at the ceiling, said nothing. "Rape and assault. He must have been a sweet character," I said, trying to get back to Thomas.

"That was a joke—the rape part. Porky Thomas never had to rape May Russell."

"Porky?" This wasn't down on my data sheet.

"He was always hungry as a kid. He'd eat anything, like a pig. But why talk of him? He just got what a black boy gets every day if he steps out of 'line'—framed. Did you buy your Jaguar in England?"

"No." I wondered what she meant by Thomas being framed. "Did Porky...?"

"I thought maybe you'd traveled abroad with a band. I'm saving for a trip to Europe. My favorite daydream."

"That's one thing we have over the ofays; leaving the States is more of a joy for us."

Her eyes sparkled. "Have you been abroad?"

"Paris, Berlin, Rome, Leghorn.* I was a captain in the army,"†
I said, talking too much. "What did you mean by saying Thomas
was framed?"

"A captain—well! I wanted to join the WACs once, to travel.
How is Paris, *really,* how is it?"

"Wonderful. Look, about—"

"Imagine being able to walk anyplace without even wondering if you're welcome. Seeing your car set me dreaming again.
Those bucket seats, they're so different."

"Care to take a ride? Any place we can stop for a drink?"

"Thank you but I don't want to take a ride," she said, but I
knew she did. "There is an after-hours shack out in the country
where they sell bootleg stuff. But it's a depressing, dirty place."

I stood up. "Then let's just take a ride."

She didn't get up. Looking at the table she said, "No."

"Come on, I want to see the city."

"At night? No, Mr. Jones, it sounds too much like the well-
dressed city smoothie giving the country-bumpkin gal a break."

"What?" I laughed. "I'm not going to make a pass at you. Not
that you aren't pretty, but I won't make a play. Or do you think
I will?"

"I think you're a liar, Mr. Jones." She said it softly, staring up

---

* A port city in Italy known more commonly as Livorno. Repeatedly bombed by the
Allies in World War II, it sustained heavy damage. It was "liberated" by the US Fifth
Army on July 19, 1944. The Fifth Army also was the first to enter Rome during the
war. However, the Fifth Army was not activated until 1943, in Morocco, and if Touie
was part of that army, he must have been detached from it in connection with his visit
to Berlin. His visit to London likely occurred when he was first activated; many troops
entering Europe did so through London.

---

† Although more than 1.5 million Black men and women served in American forces in
World War II, Black officers were unusual, restricted to serving in Black units. The only
Black combat unit to fight in Europe was the 92nd Infantry Division, which was indeed
part of the Fifth Army. That Touie served in the 92nd is made evident by his receipt of
the Silver Star, which he mentions later—the medal is only awarded for valor *in combat.*

at me with bold eyes. "You told Pop you were driving all yesterday, why should you want to drive some more? You talk of New
Orleans and Chicago but your car has New York plates. Exactly
what are you doing in Bingston?"

"I told you, merely resting…"

"I know what you told us."

I didn't know what to say; wondered why I was suddenly
frightened of this young girl. I stood there like a dummy for
a second, then for no reason I pulled out my wallet, asked,
"Should I pay you now for…?"

Her eyes stopped me, although she didn't say a word for a
moment; then she said, "Oh…put your damn money away!
Do you think I'm asking because I'm afraid you'll run out on
your bill? Maybe you're right, money-grubbing is another
small-town hobby. My God, Pop and Mom, they just sock
it away.…All the time I was a kid, even when I was in high
school, I rarely saw Mom. She was cooking and busting suds
in a white house, even bringing home leftover food for us.
And Pop making as much as anybody else in town!"

She looked away and I stood there, liking Frances, feeling
sorry for her—and still afraid. She broke the awkward silence
with "You can stay here the night but I want you to leave in
the morning. You're not a drummer. I'm a jazz nut, and I know
the name of every bandman in the country. I don't believe you
came up from New Orleans in that Jaguar: if you'd been in the
deep South you never would have walked into the drugstore
acting like you wanted to slug Mr.—the cop. Pop told me
about that."

"I seem to have been quite a conversation piece," I said,
thinking I had no choice now, I *had* to trust her before she asked
too many questions.

"Any stranger causes talk in a small town. You want to stay in

Bingston, that's your business. But you're also in our house and that makes it my business. All during supper you've been trying to quiz me about Porky Thomas and...Well, I even doubt your name is Jones."

"You're right. I'm Toussaint Marcus Moore from New—"

She clapped her hands and laughed, the laughter lighting up her face. "How wonderful! Marcus after Marcus Garvey, of course!"*

"Yeah. My father...naming me like that I don't have to tell you any more about him. Frances, you've made a lot of big talk about rights. I'm a private detective—there's a colored man being framed for the Thomas killing back in New York. That's why I'm here. I need help badly—your help."

She stood up. "A private eye?"

I flashed my badge.

"I'll be glad to help in any way I can, Toussaint...Touie."

I said cautiously, "Wait up. Something else you have to know—it won't be safe or easy. Remember I said a colored man is being framed for the murder. I certainly won't involve you, but at the same time helping me is...messy."

"I don't care, I'll—" The bitterness came back to her face abruptly. *"You?"*

I nodded. "The New York City police are looking for *a* Negro they found with Thomas' body. That's me; I was there. You have to believe I didn't do it. New York or down in Cotton Patch Corners,† when a black man is found around a body it's all the same—he's guilty."

---

* Garvey (1887–1940) was a Jamaican-born American union organizer and founder of the Universal Negro Improvement Association. He was a vocal Black nationalist and, as a leader of the pan-African movement, advocated the establishment of separate-but-equal Black nations around the world, notably, Liberia.

† A proverbial small Southern town, like Podunk.

She was staring at me with wide eyes. "But you're a detective."

"I was shadowing Thomas. Frances, I think the answer to the killing has to be in Bingston. I have about twenty-four hours to come up with the answer before 'a' Negro is known to be me. Still want to help?"

She was looking at me as if she was about to cry. Then she turned and started stacking the dishes in the sink. I waited a moment, feeling sick. I said, "Okay, I don't blame you. But give me one break, don't tell anyone what I've—"

"I'd like to take that ride now. I'll get my coat."

I went upstairs and got my coat and hat. Frances was waiting at the door dressed in a plain cloth coat that looked baggy and worn, an ugly woolen stocking cap on her head. A door opened upstairs and Mrs. Davis stuck her gray head over the banister, asked, "Where are you going, Fran?"

"Mr. Jones is taking me for a ride," she said, opening the front door.

"At this hour? Fran, I want to talk to you for a—"

"Mama, it's perfectly all right. Go to bed, please. We'll be back soon."

Outside it was cold and dark. Unlocking the car door I turned to look at her dark face, tried to remember a poem I'd once read about the "night being dark like me."* Then I wondered if I was being taken; perhaps the ride she meant was directly to the local police station? But somehow I trusted her—not that I had any choice.

The Jag was dirty. I'd been refused service on the trip down, and had to eat in the car. "Excuse the condition of the car. I—"

"Let's drive. It's cold." She shivered.

We got in and I backed out of the driveway and headed for

---

* Harlem Renaissance poet Langston Hughes's poem "Dream Variations" (1926) has the line "While night comes on gently, dark like me."

noplace, just drove. I opened the heater. After a long silence Frances asked, "Can you tell me what happened, Touss... Touie?"

"Sure. I want to. All started three days ago—seems like a lifetime now. But three days ago I was sitting in my office..."

THREE DAYS AGO

2

It started out as a big day—although I had no idea as I made up my studio bed, turning my room into my "office," how big a day it was going to be.

I share an old-fashioned railroad flat* with a fireman named Ollie and a photographer called Roy, who works as a short-order cook to keep himself eating, and that's no joke. We live on the ground floor of a small semi-tenement up in what is stupidly known as Sugar Hill.† It's a good deal: splitting expenses three ways it costs each of us about twenty-five dollars a month, which is only slightly more than you have to pay per week for a room with "kitchen privileges" in most parts of Harlem. I have the front room, which doubles as my office, a simple but dignified sign in the window stating I am a licensed PRIVATE INVESTIGATOR. Both Ollie and Roy are younger than I, and over the weekend the place is full of girls and music. Not that I play the chick field; Sybil is about all the girl I can handle, or want to.

---

* A dwelling with a series of rooms connecting to each other in a straight line, as if on rails, like compartments on a passenger train.

---

† A Harlem neighborhood filled with Victorian mansions; by the 1950s, many had been converted into multifamily dwellings.

Ollie was working a morning tour and being a sucker for horses had left six bucks on my desk with instructions for me to play a nag called Dark Sue across the board. I had the alarm set for seven, not because I had to get up for a job, but to move my car to the other side of the street, a daily game between me and the cops since they put in this alternate-side-of-the-street parking. I showered and had coffee and juice with Roy, finally found a parking space on Amsterdam Avenue, considered washing the Jaguar but figured another day's dust wouldn't hurt. I hate to be mistaken for these clowns who spend every free minute polishing their cars, take better care of them than they do of themselves. I stopped off at the delicatessen, bought some milk and bread, and put in Ollie's bet; and on a hunch put down two bucks on the horse to show, for myself. The delicatessen always amazed me; although it was only a front for the numbers syndicate,* the gray-haired white guy who ran it kept it spotless and well stocked, actually had it a going business—as a delicatessen.

Back in my room I dusted my modernistic furniture, which still looked pretty good, turned on the radio, and read my mail. There was a statement from the bank; my special checking account was down to sixty bucks. There was a mimeographed letter from the Post Office Department informing me I had been reached on the mail carrier's list and had two weeks in which to tell them if I wanted the job or not. There was an ad, and a letter from a downtown agency, my former boss, Ted Bailey, giving me a skip-tracing job. He always gave me the "colored" cases. I never knew if he was afraid of the various Harlems throughout

---

* The numbers syndicate was a gang-controlled gambling operation in which bets were placed on a random number publicly announced. In New York, the number was generally the last three digits of the betting handle at the major racetracks, announced in daily horse-racing publications and other newspapers. Although Italian mobs generally controlled these operations, there were Black syndicates as well.

New York City* or was merely throwing business my way. But
I never got a "white" skip-tracing case. A woman named James
had bought a combination stove and refrigerator for $320, on
time of course, paid in $150 and then left her job and last known
address, taking the stove-refrigerator.

So that was the mail. I put the letter from Ted in my pocket,
read a morning paper Roy had brought in the night before, and
wondered what I'd do about the P.O. job. I didn't want to take it
but if I told Sybil that she'd raise sand. While I was thinking this
over, I glanced out the window—my blinds needed dusting—
and saw a cab stop and a woman get out. She didn't look like
she belonged on 147th Street. Not because of the slightly bewildered way she looked around, or because she was white with
delicate copper-colored hair cut short in an Italian bob snugly
about her head; but because she was dressed like midtown Park
Avenue. Her clothes were simple, but smart and expensive; her
slim figure and handsome face had been given a lot of care—
every day. She walked into the hallway and a moment later there
was a knock on my door. When I opened it she slowly ran her
cool eyes over my hulk, lingering for a long second at my busted
nose. She actually pushed past me, walking with a kind of show-
girl strut around the room. "You Mr. T. M. Moore?" she asked,
talking out of the side of her thin mouth.

"That's right."

"Can you be bought? Will you double-X me?"

"What?" She didn't look like a loon.

"Will you sell me out to the first bubble-belly dame who
crosses your path? I'm in a jam, see? With a statuesque blonde

---

* There were many ethnic neighborhoods in New York City, widely separated.
"Harlem," for example, consisted of Black Harlem and "Spanish" Harlem (East
Harlem, known as "El Barrio"). There were also Chinese, Italian, Irish, and Jewish
neighborhoods.

who's been had by a redhead, also statuesque, see? But the mastermind is a gray-headed babe who only is Junoesque—on her father's side. Ya got the angle, Mac?"* She strode over to me and slapped my chest and hips. "What, no rod? You can be reported to the private optic union for not packing a rod."

"Stop reaching, lady. It's too early for cornballing. What do you want?"

She smiled; her teeth were very white and even and she couldn't have been more than thirty-two. In a crisp, controlled voice she said, "Please excuse me, Mr. Moore. This is my first time in a detective's office and I simply couldn't resist the gag."

I didn't get the joke but I sat behind my desk, very businesslike, pointed to my Swedish plywood chair as I told her, "Have a seat."

"Thank you. I approve of your furniture: modern but in low key. My name is Kay Robbens, with an 'e'. Sid Morris recommended you." She crossed her long legs and smiled again. She didn't have to say she was enjoying herself, that being in a Negro's office was kicks to her.

I relit my pipe slowly, careful *not* to look at her legs, asked, "Are you in need of a private detective?"

She nodded. Her eyes were faintly made up, a delicate blue on the lids; everything about her face was delicate, maybe even pretty on second look. She took a whiff of my pipe smoke, said, "Lovely spicy odor. What is it?"

"London Dock."

"Can I borrow some?" She pulled a tiny jeweled pipe out of her bag and I pushed my tobacco pouch across the desk without batting an eye. She wasn't Park Avenue, she was Eighth Street.†

---

* Kay is parodying the style of the popular private eye novels of the day, epitomized by Mickey Spillane's novels such as *I, the Jury* (1947).

† In the 1950s, Eighth Street, in Greenwich Village, was a Bohemian, artistic neighborhood; by the 1960s, it had become commercialized, a tourist attraction.

Sucking on her little pipe she said, "This is nice. Any special store?"

"You can buy it most anyplace. Did Sid recommend my tobacco?"

She slipped me that smile again, sure it was dazzling me, suddenly stood up and walked over to look at my army discharge framed on the wall, the little glass showcase atop my books holding my Bronze Star and Silver Star. She even glanced at my books, then sat down again, openly staring at me over her pipe.

The act was getting a trifle boring. "Thinking of starting your own army?" I asked, wondering how she kept her blue eyes so clear and bright.

"I'm thinking of hiring you as a detective, only I must be absolutely certain of one thing   whether you take the job or not, whatever I tell you now must remain in the strictest confidence. Agreed?"

"I respect the confidence of all my clients."

"Good. I like the way you look. If I hire you it will be for a minimum of one month. I can pay fifty dollars a day, plus moderate expenses."

She said it easily; I tried hard to play it cool but—fifteen hundred dollars!* I sat up straight, as if I'd been pulled erect, and managed to say casually, "Depends upon what you expect me to do. Has to be legit."

"This is a shadowing job. I must know where a...somebody...is all the time. It will be your job to see that he stands still, that I can put my hands on him any time I wish."

I glanced at the thick wedding ring on her left hand. "Sounds okay, Mrs. Robbens, so far."

She knocked the ashes out of her pipe and took a deep

---

* Equal to more than $25,000 in 2021 wages according to Williamson, Measuring Worth, 2021.

breath. Her bosom was small and compact. "Here we go, and remember, this must be top secret. I'm in the Press Information Department of Central Televising. At the moment I'm assigned as P.R. to a new show due to premiere shortly. It's to be called *You—Detective!* and will be carried full net across the country. It's a big-budget show. We rehash some unknown but factual crimes, and offer a reward if any viewer can nab the criminal. It's been done before; you've probably seen similar shows."

"If it's been done before, why start another one?"

She laughed, real tinkling laughter, as if she were fifteen. "Mr. Moore, everything has been done before, it's *how* you do it that makes the selling difference. Our sponsor is a bug on criminals and detectives. A bug with a large drug company and a top advertising budget, so we've been kicking this crime-detective format around for a long time. It will be on film and we already have several shows in the can. Briefly, the idea is we dig up little-known crimes—gory or sexy ones—show the actual scenes of the crime, interview some of the people involved, the police, flash some of the 'wanted' flyers on the TV screen. The narrator is an actor with a rugged square chin like Dick Tracy.* He'll be known as the Chief Inspector, and he ends the show by rehashing the clues, adds a few hints from his 'stoolies,' and finally points a thick finger at the audience as he orders his staff to *get* the fugitive. All corny as hell, isn't it?"

I didn't know whether to nod or not. I shrugged.

"We have quite an audience-participation deal worked out: with two box tops one gets a small badge and a lot of other hocus-pocus. If a person with a badge sends in information that leads to an arrest, or reports it to the police, he gets double the

---

* The hero of the popular detective comic strip created by Chester Gould in 1931.

reward a nonbuyer will receive. In short, it is a combination adventure and giveaway show."*

"And makes everybody a stool pigeon."

Mrs. Robbens wrinkled up her thin nose. "It's low level, moronic, disgusting…and my job."

"Where do I come in? Am I supposed to dig up cases for the show?"

"No, we have all we need, for now. You're to—" She suddenly noticed Ollie's scratch sheet on my desk, snapped her fingers as she glanced at the expensive watch on her bony wrist. "May I phone my bookie? I have a hunch running in the fourth race."

She reached across the desk and took my phone before I could say yes or no, dialed somebody named Jack, told him, "This is Kay. I'd like a five-dollar lunch delivered at four. If I'm not around leave it on my desk. I'm busy on a story called Fast Bunny that looks like a winner. Okay? Thanks." I had a feeling this was an act strictly for my benefit, although I didn't know why she had to impress me. I puffed on my pipe and looked at the sheet; the opening odds on Fast Bunny were 6 to 1.

Putting the phone back she slipped me the cool smile again. "It's silly. Butch and I spend hours at night doping the races, then I usually forget to place a bet in time. Where were we?"

"At where I come into the picture."

"I'm sorry, I should have explained that first. As I told you, I'm public relations on the show. We have quite a publicity gimmick in the making. On the third week of the show we will use the case of Robert Thomas, wanted by the Ohio police for raping and assaulting a poor sixteen-year-old kid. A brutal crime

---

* Lacy was ahead of his time in creating such a show. Detectives were popular on television in the 1950s, but true crime shows (such as the long running *Cops*) were decades away. Audience participation was well established, especially for children's television, though Lacy's idea of the audience as "stool pigeons" is novel.

that took place about six years ago. He's living and working here in New York under the name of Richard Tutt. You're to keep tabs on him."

"What does 'tabs' mean to you?"

"For the next week or two, until his case is televised, all you do is check that he's on his job every day, that he doesn't move. Won't be much work. However, from the second his 'wanted' flyer is flashed on TV screens, you're to tail him twenty-four hours a day—until we rap him, which will be—"

"Until you do what?"

Her face showed surprise. "Rap him, send him up. That's the big publicity deal. A few hours after his case is shown we have a stooge set to turn Tutt in to the police, claiming it was all a result of our show. I don't have to blueprint the rest; our sponsor does a great deal of advertising, we'll make every paper in the nation and be able to have the stooge planted on several TV news programs. I'm counting on the publicity to shove the show into a top rating."

"How did you learn where Thomas is now?"

"We do a thorough research job on all cases. One of our writers—he practically originated the show—got the data on Thomas. We used his case to audition the show, as a matter of fact. Now you understand your job: keep Thomas in sight until we're ready to lower the boom on him."

"This Thomas…is he…I mean, is he colored?"

She looked startled. "Oh no. If anything, he's a Southern cracker."

I'd been on "white" cases before. I mean, I worked every Friday and Saturday as a special doing guard work in a department store where Sid was the personnel manager. Still, my being an all-day tail in a white neighborhood raised a few obstacles. But for fifteen hundred dollars—hell, I'd make a good try

at jumping over the Empire State Building. Only it was odd that
Central Telecasting—she—hadn't gone to one of the big detective outfits.

Mrs. Robbens guessed my thoughts and said, "I came to you
for two reasons. In a large agency there might be a leak and I
don't have to tell you that if this reaches the papers ahead of
time the publicity will blow up in our faces and ruin the show.
So a one-man agency was needed. You were recommended to
me, and I feel I can count on your discretion, even after the case
is ended. From time to time we have various matters needing
investigation at the studio, and this can very well be your entree
to Madison Avenue. I always try to give you people a helping
hand, so very frankly I was pleased when I learned you were a
Negro." The smile again, on the patronizing side this time.

Okay, whites can sure say the jerkiest things and I'd met her
type before. At least she was jerky in a friendly way; too many of
them are nasty jerks.

"Will you take the case?"

"I think so," I said, as if I was considering it.

She opened her bag and took out a thin but beautiful pile of
twenty-dollar bills. "Here's three hundred dollars as a retainer.
Now, for the time being this is hush-hush, even in our office.
Only my immediate boss knows about the arrest and publicity
angle. Matter of fact, I'm paying you out of petty cash. You're not
to phone me at Central unless it's something terribly urgent. I'm
in the phone book and...Here's my home phone and address.
Call me at home every night. At about eight."

"Why every night?"

"From now on it will be the only contact I'll have with you.
You don't have to go into detail, merely that things are okay.
However, even over my home phone you're never to say you
are a detective. In TV one never knows when a phone is tapped.

Everything crystal clear, Mr. Moore? What does 'T. M.' stand for, by the bye?"

"It doesn't stand for 'by the bye,'" I wisecracked, "but for Toussaint Marcus, Mrs. Robbens."

"What a charming name. Toussaint. After the Haitian patriot?" *

"Aha. My father was a student of Negro history, Mrs. Robbens."

"While we're on the name bit, it happens to be *Miss* Robbens. I shall call you Toussaint and you may call me Kay."

"Let me call you what I want," I said, wondering about the "Miss" angle. She was sporting a thick wedding ring but perhaps on Madison Avenue it was better politics to be single.

"Shall we be on our way, Toussaint?"

"Keep it down to Touie, please. Where are we going?"

"Downtown. This is the address of the freight company that employs Thomas. I'll point him out, you take the ball from there."

"Fine." Happily my portable† wasn't in hock and I typed out a receipt. As I put on my coat I went down the hall to Ollie's room; since he was civil service the apartment was in his name. I left eighty dollars in his drawer with a note saying I was paying up the two months' back rent I owed, and the balance was against future rent.

As we stepped outside a couple of cats hanging around the stoop gave us the eye, but quietly. Miss Robbens said, "We'll take a cab. About your expense account, don't overdo the padding. Be different if Central had hired you directly, but I—"

"Don't worry about it," I said, walking her over to my Jag,

---

* Toussaint Louverture (1743–1803), now known as the "father of Haiti," was the dominant figure of the Haitian Revolution at the end of the eighteenth century.

† Touie means his portable typewriter.

which left her speechless—for once. I tooled across 145th Street toward the West Side Highway, thankful I had gas. In the bucket seat her skirt fell away, showing thin thighs and sexy black garters. We both glanced at her legs for a split second. I told myself I'd have to make crystal certain she understood what I was being paid for. Not that I was too interested—Sybil had far better stems.

In the fifteen or twenty minutes it took us to reach Forty-first Street she told me—for no reason—all about her unhappy first marriage, even how lousy her husband had been in bed. I listened politely, wanting to tell her it takes two to be good or bad in the hay. But I kept my mouth shut.

"...The kind of male slob who objected to my having a career. Career! It's a job. What he refused to understand was that in this world of nobodies, everybody has the yen to be a somebody. I'm sure you know that."

"I'm afraid to even try to think about it."

She turned in the low seat abruptly, showing more pale white thigh. "Don't ever make fun of me! I can't stand that; it's the height of rudeness!"

"I'm not making fun of you, Miss Robbens. And—"

"I told you to call me Kay."

"And pull your skirt down. I've seen legs before, Kay."

She didn't move, sat in silence for a minute. As I cut off the highway she asked, "Why did you buy a Jaguar, Touie?"

"As you said, everybody wants to be a somebody," I told her, cleverly, I thought. I checked the freight-company address in my notebook. It would be a waste of time trying to find free parking space, so I turned into a parking lot, paid the man a buck. Miss Robbens showed a lot of leg getting out but I knew that wasn't what the white attendant was staring at.

It was eleven fifteen when we reached the freight company.

She said, "Thomas comes out for lunch at noon. We have plenty of time and I'm hungry."

"Nothing but joints around here."

"I don't mind," she said, walking toward Eighth Avenue and into one of those overgrown bars that's a combination cafeteria and gin mill. There were some dozen men at the bar and tables, all of them white, of course. We gathered another round of "looks" as we got a couple of greasy hamburgers, beers, found a table. Two characters dressed like truckers were at a table near us, and one of them, a lardy redhead in his late twenties, began talking about us in a husky whisper. I didn't have to hear to know what he was saying.

Robbens was enjoying herself, babbling about places like this giving her a "refreshing sense of balance." I kept an eye on Red because you never know what some whites will do. They might even kill you.

We finished our beers and Miss Robbens pulled the string—she *had* to smoke her pipe. We were a circus sensation now. Red snickered and he and his pal laughed too loudly at something which had as a tag line "…she must like it."

When Kay glanced at their table and wrinkled her nose as if smelling something rotten, I knew I was in for action, going to earn my dough the hard way. Usually I let most of that slop in one ear and out the other, but now I couldn't have my client's confidence in me shaken. Also I was steamed, at both Red and my client.

While I was wondering how I'd make my play, Red obliged by getting up for coffee. As he was returning to his table, I told Miss Robbens loudly, "I'll get you some water."

"I don't want any…."

Pretending to look back at Kay, I walked into Red—hard. He weighed about 170, and my 234 pounds sent him flat on the dirty floor. Unfortunately he didn't spill the coffee over himself—only on the floor.

I said, "Sorry, old clumsy me," and picked him up. I lifted him off the floor and onto his feet, squeezing the hell out of his arms, working my thumbs into his muscle. It looked as though I was lifting him with ease, but I had my legs set, was straining. He tried to move his numb arms and couldn't as he said, "Why don't you watch it?"

"I told you it was an accident," I said slowly, waiting to see what he was going to do, watching his buddy at the table, too.

Red wasn't sure of himself; he'd taken a rugged fall. He decided not to do anything. Brushing himself off he said, "Lost a cup of java, too...."

I tossed a dime on the counter. "Give sonny a refill," and continued on my way to the water fountain, bringing a glass back to Kay.

Knocking the ashes out of her pipe, she squeezed my hand, whispered, "A magnificent bit." She was happy as the devil.

"Look," I said, keeping my voice down, "let's get one thing settled. Don't make a civil-rights case out of everything."

"Me? Really, I fail to see where I—"

"I'm only saying when I want a cup of coffee I want coffee and not a scene. When I want to make a test case of something, I will. I'm not blaming you or anybody. Not even that redheaded sonofabitch. I'm merely making a statement."

"I don't get it."

"When you go in for food you don't think a thing about it. But me, in a white restaurant, there's always a doubt, a...Forget it."

"Forget what? Do you mean you only want to eat in Harlem restaurants?"

"Of course not. I mean, in the future, tell me what you want, food or excitement." I was about to add she had a pipe, she didn't need me *and* the pipe to attract attention. Instead, I smiled as if we'd been kidding, said in a normal voice, "Only have about ten minutes; shouldn't we be on our way?"

"Yes," she said, making a casual but smiling exit. Outside she said. "This disturbs me. I've always gone out of my way to be considerate to Negroes, but you're all so touchy."

"I always go out of my way to be nice to you people, too."

"Why must you make fun of me? I told you I don't like it."

"I'm not making fun of you—you're the one who's touchy," I told her, and told myself to shut up before she pulled me off the case. I gave her a best grin, added, "We're fighting over nothing. Let's get to work. We'll be too conspicuous standing opposite or outside the freight entrance together. Has Thomas ever seen you?"

"No. I've been quite a detective on my own. Here's all our data on him, home address, age, etc. This is a snap of him taken six years ago. He hasn't changed much, except he keeps his hair crew-cut, and it's a sandy blond now. You can pick him out from the snap, but if you want, I'll point him out.

"To be on the safe side, you might as well finger him. Look, we'll stand across the street, but not together. Soon as you see him, start walking toward the corner. I'll stop you and ask for a match. Corny, but it will do. Without looking across at him, you'll tell me what he's wearing, to be doubly certain I have the right man. Keep walking and wait for me at the corner. I'll drive you back to your office."

"Don't bother, I can take a cab. You'll phone me at my apartment around eight tonight and let me know how it's going?"

"Sure," I said, putting the papers she gave me in my pocket.

She gave me the dazzling smile again. "You've made this a most interesting morning for me."

"That's fine. People are coming out for lunch; let's get going."

We were on the fringe of the garment district and the street started to fill up, mostly with women, many of them Puerto Ricans and/or Negroes. Miss Robbens stood near the entrance of a building, looking like a model waiting for a lunch date. I leaned against the window of a small coffeepot,* packing my pipe.

Across the street, a steady stream of men and women came out of the freight-company building, which was a modest skyscraper housing a couple of dozen other concerns and dress factories. Miss Robbens walked toward me and we went through the match routine. I felt silly but as I lit my pipe she said in a fierce hammy whisper, "He's the one in the blue sweat shirt. See him?"

"Yeah. I'll phone you tonight." She walked on and I watched her stop a cab.

Thomas was an easy make, tall and wiry with a stiff, military way of holding himself and a lean sharp face—except for his lips, which were thin and almost girlish. It was an easy face to remember, those lips and the strong square jaw. He looked about twenty-five, and if his dirty-blond hair was dyed it was a good job. He was wearing dungarees, a blue sweat shirt, and work shoes. With a couple of other young fellows, he marched into a luncheonette. Crossing the street, I read the hand-written menu pasted on the luncheonette window. Thomas was sitting at the counter, blowing on a cup of coffee. He had a cigarette behind one ear and his right cheek was pockmarked.

I went to the corner and bought an afternoon paper, looked through it, and twenty minutes later walked slowly back to the luncheonette. Thomas was lounging against the counter, the

---

* A small restaurant, what might today be called a coffee shop.

cigarette pasted to his funny lips, bulling with the other guys. From the relaxed way they were leaning against the counter, they did hard physical work: looked like pugs* resting between rounds. I walked away as they came out, went across the street to lean against a parked truck and talk some more as they got a little sun. I stood in the lobby of a building, smoking my pipe and watching Thomas until he went back to work at twelve forty-five. Kay's info said he knocked off at five, leaving me free till then. Life was terrific; a month's work and I was getting it on a silver platter.

Back at the parking lot I found one of my whitewalls flat. Maybe the attendant did it because he saw a white woman with me, and maybe it was a leaky valve as he said. My rubber was old. He kept a straight face and, since the tire wasn't cut, I had him put in a new valve and air.

Sybil works as a long-lines operator,† a service assistant—a kind of foreman—and worked a split tour: 11 A.M. to 2 P.M., then back at 8 P.M. to work till 11 P.M. She liked the tour because she didn't have to get up early and actually only worked six hours although she was paid for eight. I phoned her at the public phone in the locker room, left a message with some girl that I'd pick her up at two. I called Sid to thank him for recommending me, and to get a line on Miss Robbens, but he was out.

With an hour to kill I phoned Ted Bailey, but he was busy on another skip-tracing job in the Village. I told him to be in front of his building in a few minutes, I'd drive him downtown.

When I got out of the army in '48 and went to N.Y.U. on the G.I. Bill, I told Sid I needed a part-time job and he had Bailey take me on as a weekend guard at the department store. Sid is a real sweet guy; he was a pilot and we got drunk together

---

* Pugs is slang for pugilists, boxers, not a reference to the breed of dogs.

† That is, a long-distance operator for the telephone company.

in Rome back in '45, have been friends ever since. Bailey ran a fairly big agency, used seven men in the department store, and was okay. Didn't treat me any different than the rest of his men—he was huffy with all of us. I was called back into service in '50, and when I came out in '53—lucky enough not to go to Korea—the store had its own guards. They were using one of Ted's men for the Friday and Saturday rush. Ted said it wasn't worth bothering with, gave me the job, which was how and why I started my own agency.

Ted was waiting for me; I didn't have to double-park. He dresses and looks like a fat hick. Actually he's a rough oscar* and far from stupid—as a dick. I get a bang out of the way he speaks in grunts—as if talking were a waste of time.

As he sat down beside me I saw he was still wearing old-fashioned high shoes. Ted said, "What a car for an investigator. An operator should have an ordinary buggy—nothing stands out like this. Jeez, what seats—like I'd slipped off a bar stool. Get my letter?"

"Thanks. I'll work on it tomorrow. Kind of busy now. Where do you want to go?"

"Drop me at Sheridan Square. So you're busy, Toussaint?"

He never called me Touie. "Things have picked up."

"You're lucky. Whole damn racket is changing. Today you can't make your pork chops unless you're a regular mechanical whiz, and even then you need contacts. I just hired me a kid who got busted out of engineering school."

"That's what I want to talk about. I'm thinking of expanding."

He pulled out a cigar and began chewing on it. "Expand where? Why stay in this two-bit racket? Ain't enough money in Harlem to make it worth your while."

---

* Dating back to 1905, the term means an offensive, unlikeable person. See *Partridge*, 1424.

"That's what I mean by expanding—out of Harlem."

"Naw, naw. Too many guys in the game now. No work. Divorce stuff, skip tracing, guard duty; they don't amount to a sour ball. Burns, Pinkerton, Holmes have the big guard jobs sewed up. Know why I hired this engineer, why I'm paying him as much as I take home? Only money around these days is in industrial spying. For that you need bugs and recorders and all kinds of electrical gadgets, and it adds up to nothing but a lousy overhead unless you got an 'in.'"

"Are you getting any of this industrial gravy?"

He gave his cold cigar a workout between his teeth as he said, "I'm getting the wrong end of the stick. Toussaint, in the old days, if a guy was sober and willing to put in hours, he could make a fair living, even big money if he wanted to be a rat and labor fink. Now...I got a...a small manufacturer, coming out with a new cheap line. His success will depend on when a competitor, the big company in the business, puts their product on the market. You see, if my boy comes out first, the big company can undersell him, so he has to catch them when they're in full production and no time to cut his throat. All he can pay is a lousy grand."

"What's lousy about a thousand bucks?"

"What I'm trying to tell you, it don't mean nothing no more. Takes me a week and plenty of dough to find out where one of the big company's executives fruits around. Then I hire a broad to pick him up and we got her joint rigged like an electrical plant, with guys outside listening to the bed conversation. I got to pay for three nights of loving and whiskey before Lover says anything we can use. The nut comes out to over nine hundred bucks—where's my pork chops?"

"Why did you take it?"

"Had to; only way to get in with these industrial big boys.

You should see the bunk I give out with—make a presentation, everything typed up with wide margins, in an expensive folder. This guy, he plays golf with a real big boy, washing-machine manufacturer who's interested in learning about the new models due next year. But you see me on a skip-tracing deal now, still hustling for a lousy ten bucks. Pull over there, in front of the cigar store. I'll blow."

I double-parked and Ted got out, straightened his clothes and cursed my bucket seats. Then he said, "You're still young enough to get in something else. If there ain't nothing in the racket for us wh—downtown boys, what's in it for you?"

"I'm doing okay."

"Sure, for this month. And next month you're bouncing drunks at dances for pennies. Toussaint, hop on that case I gave you."

"I will. Keep your blood pressure down, Ted."

I drove down to Canal Street and parked outside the phone building, lit my pipe. Miss Robbens said the TV studio had other work for investigators; if I buttered her up, remained her pet Negro for a while—how much of it could I get? Ted had said the main thing was contacts; she could be that. First thing I had to do was move out of my bedroom-office, put up a big-time front. It would cost but it was worth the gamble.

Sybil came out with a group of women and as usual she liked the idea of my Jaguar waiting for her, the impression we both made on the other women—all of them white. Although my darkness was a real "problem" to Sybil, with the phone-company white girls she made a point of giving me a big fat kiss whenever I picked her up, as if to prove she was a Negro and proud of it, and all that.

Opening the door, I watched her walk toward the car, the sway of her solid hips. I hadn't seen her for two days and now she had a blond streak in her auburn hair—the newest style. It looked phony on her.

Sybil was what my old man used to call "tinted whites": her skin was a creamy white and her hair was "good" (an expression that used to make the old man mount his soapbox at once). I suppose Sybil could have easily "passed." She had the kind of color and features that if you saw her in Harlem you'd assume she was "colored." If you saw her downtown you might think she was Spanish, if you thought about it at all. When I was out with Sybil I often collected the same kind of "looks" I'd picked up with Kay. I suppose the reason Sybil didn't pass was her old-fashioned ideas about color—the prestige she thought her lightness gave her in Harlem.

Sybil was a habit with me. We had been going together for about three years. Her parents were from one of the islands and when she was a kid in Washington, D.C., Sybil had tried hard to lose her accent; now she worked harder at keeping it, spoke with a kind of clipped English. She was twenty-nine years old, had married a jerk when she was a kid, worked in an aircraft factory during the war to put her husband through med school. When the army took over his education this louse divorced Sybil and married a Chicago widow who owned real estate. Sybil was a habit, as I said, and most times a very comfortable habit. We hit it off, although sometimes her phony standards made me go straight up. Like the few times I'd realized how she felt about my dark skin, or like she would never come to my room, although Roy and Ollie knew all about us.

We kissed, her mouth cool, a good smell of perfume about her. "This is a surprise, Touie."

Cutting across Canal to the highway, I said, "I was downtown on a case. A big fish, honey. I'm going to make fifteen hundred dollars!" As we raced up the highway, the Hudson rough and cold looking, I told her as much about the case as I could. Then my ideas about opening a real office downtown, perhaps going to school for a month or so to learn about these electrical gadgets.

Sybil thought I ought to pay up my debts, bank the rest, forget my big ideas. But of course she was thrilled about me getting the dough and we were doing fine—when I made two mistakes. I mean driving along the Hudson in my Jag, a fine-looking chick beside me, I really felt like a success boy...until I was kidding about Miss Robbens' pipe. And as with Kay, the low seat of the Jaguar caused Sybil's skirt to fall back, show her strong thighs. I reached over and squeezed them, said she sure had it all over the Madison Avenue babes. Sybil tucked her skirt tightly around her legs, said, "I'm not interested in her legs. You know I don't like that kind of dirty talk."

"For the love of—what's *dirty* about it? Only the two of us here and we've certainly—"

"Touie!"

"Sybil, sometimes you act like a silly, prissy—"

"Touie Moore, I've told you before about talking like that."

"Yeah, you have," I said, wanting to add "Too damn many times." Instead I shut up.

We reached her brownstone basement one-room "apartment"—with a view of the river, if you stuck your head far enough out the window to break your neck (and for which she was paying seventy-two dollars a month). As I took off my coat and tie, I mentioned the post-office deal. That tore it.

"Oh Touie darling!" Sybil said, putting everything she had into a big hug. "That's the *real* news. When do you start?"

"I don't know," I said, kissing her, running my hands through her soft hair. And wondering, for no damn reason, how many generations of rape it took to produce her creamy skin. "I don't even know if I'm going to take it."

I felt her tighten up before she stepped back out of my arms. "Why not? It's civil service, what we've always talked about."

"Sure, S.O.P.* for a Negro. That's why they call the main post office Uncle Tom's Cabin.† Sybil, honey, this TV contact changes things. This is my big chance to start a real agency."

"You sound like a little boy infatuated with private eyes," she said coldly, taking off her coat. She was wearing a simple striped blouse and skirt that showed off her chunky figure. Sybil was very style conscious, mainly because she had this crazy idea a colored woman had to *prove* she knew how to dress. The trouble was, often the "latest" styles weren't intended for Sybil's solid figure.

Hanging up my jacket I took out my wallet. "How much do I owe you, honey?"

She pulled back the Japanese screen from the kitchenette, started the coffee working. "Thirty-five dollars."

I gave her fifty bucks extra. "Buy yourself something."

Very pleased, she thanked me with a tiny kiss, pocketed the money, and went on with her cooking. I started on my special-ty—a tossed salad.

She put on eggs and sausages, humming to herself. I knew exactly how her mind was working. As if I were an excited kid that needed cooling off, a moment later she said, "Touie, this is your big opportunity, so let's not talk nonsense. You'll sub for a few years, but even so, you'll be making about four thousand, and what

---

* Military slang, meaning "Standard Operating Procedure."

---

† The US Post Office was, by 1960, the largest employer of Black workers in the United States. See "African-American Postal Workers in the 20th Century," US Postal Service, https://about.usps.com/who-we-are/postal-history/african-american-workers-20thc .htm.

with my job we can easily afford a new apartment, perhaps in the houses being built on 125th Street, interracial, too. We'll buy all new furniture, and a new car. Or a house out in St. Albans with—"

"What's wrong with my Jag?"

"Nothing, but in time we'll buy a new one. Darling, this is security, you know that as well as I do."

"A top detective agency, that can mean real folding money."

"All right, get it out of your system, talk about it. Be honest, dear, you only got into the detective business by chance. What do you *really* know about it?"

"Told you, one of the things I'm going to use the dough for, study up on these electrical things. Hon, the private-eye business has changed. Now it's finding out for CBS what new programs NBC has in mind. Big-money stuff. Ted Bailey gave me the lowdown today."

"I suppose these big concerns are waiting to give the business to you—a black boy?"

"Seems to me I landed this new assignment just because I am colored." I don't like light-skinned people, even Sybil, calling me black.

"Touie Moore, all the time I've known you, you've been rubbing pennies together. If you weren't living in that dump with those other two studs, you'd have been on the street most of the time. Only real job you have is that department-store weekend thing, gives you a great big twenty a week. Bouncer, guard— how degrading can you get? Let's face it, you paid tax on seventeen hundred dollars last year. I never could understand why you insist on sticking to your badge. You're personable, well dressed, you could have made double that as a sales clerk. You told me yourself this Sid offered you such a job. But no, Dick Tracy has to keep on playing cops and robbers."

"At least my time was my own, and now it's going to pay off."

"What time was your own? Staying up all night at dances, holding up drunks, getting vomited on? You took all these civil-service exams because you know in your heart detective work is a blind alley."

I set up the bridge table as she took out the dishes, opened a bottle of beer. "Sybil, I'm not saying it's been easy, or that I can make it. But neither am I rushing into carrying mail for the rest of my life. I want to think it over, carefully."

"Go ahead, but there's nothing to think about. And let's not argue while we eat. It's bad for the digestion."

We ate listening to radio music and I was mixed up. I could understand her point; hell, she'd been making triple my income for years. Still, I couldn't dismiss the agency idea as if Miss Robbens had never been in my office.

While I washed the dishes Sybil went into the large closet she called a dressing room, and which at one time had been the pantry of the house. I was sitting on the couch, lighting my pipe, when Sybil stepped out in a long lacy nothing, modeling it for my benefit. She came over, tipping like a Maltese kitten, sat on my lap, gently pulled the pipe from my mouth and planted a long hot kiss.

Sybil and I were most compatible, but now it left me cold. I was getting the full treatment, very full. I lifted her off my lap, dropped her beside me. Her eyes were big with surprise, maybe mocking me. I said, "Let's talk sense. You see, honey, another thing I thought we could do with the money is get married."

"We'll get married the day you're appointed a regular carrier."

I puffed on my pipe hard. If you can't get a doctor or undertaker, marry a civil-service worker, live in the installment rut. "I asked you to marry me a year ago; why did you say no? Be honest."

"I wasn't sure I was in love with you."

"Honey, you haven't been seeing any other John, so that sounds phony to me. Was it because I'm dark?"

She shrugged. "Touie, what are you trying to make me say? All right, when I first knew you, I admit I didn't like the idea you were dark. But that certainly wasn't why I turned you down, why I'm doing it now. Touie, you know how hard it is for our people to land decent jobs, and when one does, she has to be careful—so many men want to marry her for a meal ticket."

"That's crap."

"Touie Moore, don't you talk like that in *my* house! And it isn't b.s. You know what I went through with my louse of a husband. Seems when a man can't find himself, he finds me. I don't want—"

"I'm not your ex-husband."

"And I never want you to be. Suppose we married now, you'd move in here and long as I kept my job you could play detective the rest of your life. I'm not saying you're lazy, Touie, because you're not. But we'd never get anyplace."

"Where's 'anyplace,' Sybil?"

"You know what I mean; with a steady double income, we can live well. Touie, you're almost thirty-five. It's time you settled down. I know, the war ruined your chances for professional football, and the five or seven years you were an army officer—a nice vacation. This is the first civil-service job you've been called for; you simply can't pass it up!"

"You sound like I'm on relief."

"You want honest talk? You aren't far from relief. Ollie carries your rent, I feed you. The Jaguar, the good clothes—that's all an empty front."

That hit me like a jab to the gut. "And what the devil is living in a swank apartment, joining these dicty* social clubs, the drunken dances, but a front? Sybil, the main thing is our being together. Marriage has to be more than a money partnership."

"Movie dialogue, Touie, white movie dialogue. What's wrong in wanting to live in a *new* apartment? God knows I've lived in enough old rooms and run-down flats!"

"Nothing. I'm sick of hand-me-down apartments too. If my agency goes over big, if we give it a chance, we could live like that."

"That's a dream; a post-office check is real." She yawned, raised her arms and stretched, and under the lace gown her plump little breasts moved with a soft lazy motion. "Don't argue, Touie. My goodness, if it makes you happy, keep the detective agency going in your spare time."

I was too restless to sit, I walked around the room, flexing my muscles. The trouble was, Sybil was right; I did have a romantic conception of marriage. Still, she was making it too much cold turkey—now that I had the P.O. job she'd let me in as a full partner.

Sybil was watching me through half-closed eyes. With a cat-like movement she stretched out on the couch, her arms under her head. "Think it over for a day or two; you'll see I'm right. Come here, muscles. Come over here."

It was too corny. "I'm too tense for sleep."

She gave me a knowing smile that said I was being silly; that I knew I'd come to her. "Then get me a cover. I'll get some sleep. I'm working overtime tonight."

I covered her with a blanket, turned and walked over to the window. She called me once, softly, then a few minutes later she was sleeping. Sybil could sleep any time. I swung the TV around, tuned it in low, watched some overbright comic for a

---

* In *Harlemese*, Fisher spells the word "dickty" and defines it as "swell." As a noun, it means a "high-toned person" (298).

while. I felt lousy. Maybe it wasn't love, but I wanted to marry her. Was it wrong to also expect some sparkle instead of a merger of salary checks? Was that kid stuff? Might even take a honeymoon when Sybil had her vacation, fly out to L.A. and see my mother, who was living with my older sister and the stuffed-shirt dentist she'd married.

I went over to Sybil's dresser, got some stationery, wrote Ma a short letter, enclosed two twenties—first time *I'd* sent her money in a year. I didn't have a stamp. I quietly went through Sybil's bag and found one. At four I washed up, considered shaving, changed my shirt, and took off. After making sure the Jaguar was locked, I rode the subway downtown. I had to take Robert Thomas home and put him to bed, and it's impossible to tail anybody with a car in New York City.

I was in a real funk. It wasn't just thinking about Sybil that made me so blue. Another faint thought had been knocking at the back of my mind all afternoon: I'd always drawn the line at fink work and here I was…doing what? A lousy human bloodhound tracking a joker who had jammed himself years ago but seemed to have straightened out. I was getting set to send him to jail.…For the sake of justice? No, in order to sell more cereal or pimple cream, or whatever this TV sponsor peddled.

3

Tailing a person in a five-o'clock rush is candy. Thomas was wearing an old windbreaker over his blue sweat shirt and a knitted cap. He was in a big rush. After grabbing a fast sandwich and cup of coffee at the same dump where he ate lunch, he actually ran to the subway. It was packed and I let myself be crushed into the same car he was riding, but at the other end. Looking over the heads of the other passengers, I kept the knit cap in view.

Thomas-Tutt wasn't going home. He got off at downtown Brooklyn and raced up the steps of an old squat building that was dark except for the lights of a trade school on the second floor. Making a note of the address and time, I went across the street and leaned against a building. Almost all the nearby stores were shut and the neighborhood was quiet, empty of people— especially colored people. I got my pipe going. Although I couldn't see Thomas, I saw other young fellows working on the second floor. Some sort of electrical work; there were frequent flashes and sparks.

A young cop came by, swinging his club. He looked Italian. I tried to recall why I hadn't taken the police exam. Probably overage. He glanced at me casually and I knew what he was thinking—what's this Negro hanging around here for? Only he wasn't thinking the word Negro. If I'd been roughly dressed, he probably would have asked me.

I smoked through another pipe, thinking of Sybil, trying to clarify my thoughts about her, about us. It was after seven and I was getting tired of standing around. I didn't have to do all this, I could wait at Thomas' home address, but I wanted to know all I could about him. The cop came back, walked over to me, said, "Looks like a cold night."

"Guess it does," I said, tightening up inside, a reflex action. I didn't want to have to flash my gold badge.

"Waiting for somebody?"

I nodded.

"Maybe you don't know this neighborhood—there's an all-night stool joint a couple stores down. Be warmer."

I relaxed all at once. "Thanks. I'm waiting for a friend of mine at the school over there."

"They don't come out till eight. Welding school. Good trade to learn."

"Maybe I will wait over some coffee. Thanks, officer."

The coffeepot had a sad light in the window, which was why I hadn't noticed it before, and an even sadder-looking old man behind the counter. His face was full of wrinkles but his bald dome was tight-smooth. I sat on the first stool and ordered a hunk of pie and coffee. It was homemade pie, so I ordered the day's special—pot roast—and that was okay. I could see the school entrance across the street through the dirty window. I had another cup of coffee, paid the old man, picked up an evening paper he had on the other side of the counter. Miss Robbens' horse hadn't come in; neither had mine.

I wasn't much of a detective. While I was looking at the paper, eight o'clock came by, and Thomas and seven other young fellows came out of the school, talking loudly, and damn if they didn't head straight for this stool joint. His seeing me was the last thing I wanted but there wasn't time to get out. I motioned for a third cup of java and went on reading the paper. They trooped in, kidding the silent old man, and Thomas went to the john. When he returned there was only one empty stool—next to me, of course.

He didn't sit; instead he stood behind one of the other fellows, and ordered pie and coffee. In the dull mirror on the wall behind the counter I saw one of the students give out with a big dumb grin as he asked, "What's the matter, Tutt? Sit down, Rebel."

"Why sure, you bet I'll sit," Thomas-Tutt said, with a very slight drawl.

My shoulders and hips were never meant for counter stools, and he had to squeeze in and brush up against me even to sit down. I tried to give him room, leaned as far away from him as possible, didn't react when he dug my shoulder harder with his elbow than I thought necessary.

He was still cramped in, could hardly bring his spoon up to his mouth. He kept on grumbling, half aloud, something about "…they take over…" and the loud mouth at the other end egged him on with "You ain't eating fast, Rebel, lost your appetite?" I kept my face buried in the paper, trying to ignore them, which probably encouraged them. Finally Thomas spilled some coffee on himself, gave me a dig in the ribs as he reached over for a napkin, said in a disgusted voice, "Where Ah come from, this wouldn't happen!"

The joint was very quiet and I looked over the top of the paper, watched him take another spoonful of coffee and, with a big wink at the rest of the jerks, clumsily-on-purpose spill it on my sleeve.

It would only be worse if I didn't do something, so I stood up suddenly, knocking him against the next guy, said, "Relax, you're up North now and wearing shoes."

It was the dumbest thing I could do, but I just couldn't hold myself in. If a rumble started and that cop was called, I'd have to show my badge and that would be the end of the job. I suppose what I should have done was walk out.

There was another absolute silence; perhaps my size made Loud-Mouth stop grinning. But I'd already made the mistake; now Thomas *had* to make a play. He said, "You damn nigger!" and got up swinging his right. I caught his hand, twisted it hard behind his back, still facing his buddies. The pain made Thomas double over and when he tried to kick back at me I pulled him up sharply, then let go suddenly. He fell to the floor and his hat came off.

I said, "That wasn't smart. I have a lot of size on you. Behave and take it slow. I'm not looking for trouble."

"I'll kill you!" he said, the phony drawl gone from his voice.

"If you get up, kid, you'll get hurt."

His right hand went to his back pocket, he started to get up, then he ran his left hand through his blond hair and sat down. Big-Mouth said, "Don't get in an uproar, Mister. He didn't mean nothing."

"I know he didn't; that's why I don't want him to get up— and get hurt. Or you punks to get any childish ideas about rushing me." I tossed a dime on the counter, for the last cup of java, said, "It's all been good clean fun, fellows," and walked out.

I was so mad at myself I could have cried. Moore the super-eye, lousing up fifteen hundred bucks! But hell, I couldn't have let him call me what he did.

I walked to the subway station and it was deserted. He'd certainly spot me if I hung around there. I went out and stopped a cab. Thomas lived on West Twenty-fourth Street, according to the data Miss Robbens had given me. I had the cabbie drive me to the Twenty-third Street station. There were a lot of people around, waiting for the morning papers to come up, most of them whites. I took a plant in a dark doorway across the street from the subway entrance, made a note of the cab fare. I tried to kid myself that the coffeepot incident hadn't been too bad; I'd heard his voice and that might come in handy. But I knew how dumb I'd been. If Thomas ever spotted me again he might think I was a real cop and take a powder.* Putting on that tough act had been stupid for him too. Suppose the cops had run the both of us in, found out he was wanted? That must have been why he didn't get up, come at me with his knife.

I saw Thomas come out of the subway exit, alone. He stopped at a newsstand, talked to the old man running it, and bought a copy of *Popular Mechanics*. There was a chain cafeteria on the corner, a few stores from where I was standing. Thomas went in. He was a lad who loved to eat store food. I walked by the window. He wasn't eating but was talking to a bus girl in a white uniform. She looked about nineteen, one of these pale, delicate-looking kids you see among poor whites. Pale and delicate from not eating regularly when they were kids.

From the low, intimate way they were talking, the smile on both their faces, she could be his girl. After a few minutes he gave her hand a slight pat and left, walking up a block and into his street, then running up the steps of the small tenement that was now a ROOMING HOUSE according to an old sign over the entrance. I watched the windows but couldn't see his light. But then, I didn't know if his room was an outside one or not. I

---

* To leave, a usage first recorded in 1934 and popular in "Broadwayese" and gangster films. *Partridge*, 1537. Scholars speculate that the phrase (which was previously "take a runout powder") implied ingestion of a medicinal or laxative powder or use of a magician's vanishing powder, but its origins are uncertain.

wondered how Kay had gotten all the info, even the apartment and room number. I was sure Thomas was in for the night, would read his magazine in bed.

I went back to the cafeteria, had a glass of water. All the help had their names in plastic holders pinned to the canvas uniforms. She was Mary Burns. I crossed the street and found a phone booth in a cigar store. Of course there were a lot of Burnses, including one at a nearby address that I put down. It could be her father, her home address. It was a few minutes after nine and I phoned Miss Robbens' apartment. I heard music and voices in the background as she answered. I told her what I'd done—but not about the coffeepot trouble—and in a guarded voice she said, "You don't have to work that hard, yet. But I'm pleased you're so conscientious."

"Make things smoother when the program comes on and I really have to stick to him. Tomorrow I'll take him to work, check him again when he leaves. Call you."

"That's fine, Touie, what are you doing now?"

"Nothing."

"I have some people in, interesting folk, why don't you come up?"

"Well, I…uh…" I fingered my face. Although I only have to worry about "five-o'clock shadow" every other day, I needed a shave.

She mistook my hesitation for something else. "It's all right, these are liberal-minded people," she whispered, maybe not realizing what she was saying.

"Wasn't even thinking of *that*. I need a shave."

"Oh, forget that. Are you coming?"

"Okay." If I expected Robbens to make contacts for me on Madison Avenue, I'd have to keep in close touch with her.

Outside, without thinking, I looked around for a barbershop.

The only one I saw was closed, not that it would have mattered if it had been open. When I was nineteen I was downtown when I heard that a tobacco company was hiring Negro salesmen for summer jobs. I couldn't get a shave downtown, and by the time I went up to Harlem and back the jobs were filled. I bought a razor and blades in the cigar store, rode a bus up to Penn Station, shaved in the men's room. In the car crosstown to Miss Robbens' place on Thirty-seventh Street, I jotted down the cab fare, and as an afterthought threw in the buck I'd spent for the razor.

She lived in a remodeled brownstone, and, judging by the number of them, fixing up brownstones must be the major industry in New York City. When she buzzed the door open I took a tiny elevator I could just about get into to the third floor. Kay was waiting at the door in tight buckskin pants, a dark blue turtle-neck sweater that did a lot for her small breasts and set off her neat face and copper hair. She had a silver coin belt around her waist and odd leather slippers with tiny bells on them. She led me into a large living room done in Swedish modern, including a working fireplace, and a crazy kind of wallpaper that seemed patches of violent colors.

There was a couple on the floor before the fireplace, a guy sprawled on the couch, and a woman making a shaker of cocktails. They all stared at me with studied interest, as if they'd been boring each other before and behold, a conversation piece enters. I wondered which of the men was her husband. After she hung up my coat and hat, Kay introduced me around. The couple on the floor were man and wife and he was a writer. He was also toasting slivers of potato in the fire, using a long wooden stick, and carefully eating each sliver himself as he took it out of the flames. His name was Hank. I never did get his wife's name. The guy on the couch was named Steve McDonald and Kay said, "Steve is the current white-haired boy at Central. He originated a new show I'm doing publicity for. And last, but by no means least, this is Barbara—we share this coop."

Steve was one of these long drinks of water, with the slim build of a distance runner, and hair crew-cut so short it seemed to be painted on his narrow head. He had a habit, I saw later, of opening his eyes wide to emphasize whatever he was saying. Anyway he wasn't worrying about wrinkling his thick striped sport coat and flannel pants, lying in them.

Barbara was a trim babe with a young figure but her face looked washed out and tired and her carefully brushed hair was a silky gray all over, so it probably was a dye job. It was all wrong for her face. She said, "Hello, Touie, Kay has told me about you. Want Scotch or a hot buttered rum?"

Before I could answer Kay said, "Touie *must* try the rum."

"As you wish," Barbara said, pouring rum into a thick cup, then a slab of butter, a shake of some kind of spices. Walking to the fireplace, she knelt over Hank and swung a small copper teakettle around, poured some hot water into the cup. She was wearing a plain print dress and when she bent over her hips were lovely and full. Out of the corner of my eye I saw Steve, the couchboy, watching her hips. Then he popped his eyes at me and grinned.

I took the hot drink and Hank patted the rug beside him as he said, "Sit down. It isn't every night one can race back into history and drink with General Toussaint."

"We were in Haiti last year," his wife said.

"I'll try this," I said, sitting on a pigskin hassock.

Everybody stared at me, with friendly curiosity. I sipped my drink, which tasted like soup with a kick. Kay announced, "Touie was a captain in the army. Has medals to prove it."

"My press agent," I said, wishing she'd shut up.

Steve raised himself on one elbow, gave me a mock salute, said, "Captain, suh, the troops are in the sun. How would you like them, rare, medium, or well done?"

"You trite bastard," Barbara said.

Steve made big eyes at her. "I don't know, I thought it was pretty funny. Didn't you, Louie?"

"Not bad," I said, taking another sip of the junk in my cup.

"The name is Touie, as you very well know," Barbara said, carrying on some fight of her own with this Steve. "Like the hot rum?"

"Yeah," I lied. "I've had them before, in Paris," I added, to get in the b.s. trend.

"We were in Paris in '53," the writer's wife said, turning on the floor to face me.

There was a hi-fi phonograph set in a bookcase with a neat purring jazz record on. The writer's wife licked her lips, as if she were about to take a bite out of me, kicked the ball off with "I simply love Bessie Smith records, but they were so badly pressed; all the scratches come through on our hi-fi."

As Kay lit her pipe and sat on the floor, the writer nibbled at a blackened bit of potato and said, "I can't bear to listen to her because it galls me to remember how she died, bleeding to death and they wouldn't take her in a white hospital.* I can feel the pain in her voice."

"Her voice gets to you," Steve said.

So then I knew they were going to bat "that boy" around, as

* The legendary blues singer Bessie Smith (1894–1937) died as a result of injuries sustained in a car accident between Memphis and Clarksdale, Tennessee. After her death, jazz writer and producer John Hammond reported that the nearby White-only hospital in Clarksdale refused to treat her (*DownBeat*, November 1937, 3). This account inspired Edward Albee's 1959 one-act play, *The Death of Bessie Smith*. However, in his 2003 biography, *Bessie Smith: Empress of the Blues*, Chris Albertson identified an eyewitness account refuting this story, and Hammond's own report made it clear that he had not confirmed it with locals.

one Negro writer calls this parlor game. I mean there's a certain type of white who loves to get going on the Negro "question" or "problem," in fact feels he *must* break out into a discussion whenever he's around Negroes. I suppose talking about it is better than the attitude of most ofays who try to forget we're alive. But it had been a long long time since I'd been in this type of bull session.

Hank's wife started it by saying the Negro should migrate en masse from the South so we could use our "consolidated voting power," whatever that is.

Steve and Kay immediately jumped into the water, then Hank and Barbara wet their feet. I finished my drink, managed to make myself a plain shot instead of the warm slop I'd been sipping. I was a very quiet and polite "problem," and thought how Sybil would love this kind of b.s. As a matter of fact, they were talking so much they forgot about me—except for Barbara, who would glance at me now and then, as if watching me. Finally, as Kay finished a speech and stopped to pack her pipe, Steve popped his eyes at me and asked, "Touie, don't you believe the Negro would do better with a complete population transfer to the North?"

"I don't know," I said, which seemed to annoy everybody: I was supposed to be an expert on race relations, I guess.

Kay said, "Certainly, despite the various forms of discrimination found up here, the Negro would have a better chance, a legal chance, to fight for his rights."

"I've never been in the deep South," I said, picking my words, careful not to talk myself out of a client, "but for one thing, I doubt if the average Southern Negro has the money to move his family anyplace."

"Nonsense," Hank's wife said, her voice almost angry. "If they really wanted to, they could get away—somehow."

Kay said, "The entire history of the U.S. would have been different if the Negro had moved West right after the Civil War."

"No," Hank said, "they were promised forty acres and a mule, why should they have moved? Trouble was, the Republicans sold them out and screwed up Reconstruction."

There was another battle of words and then Kay asked, "Touie, what do you think?"

I had to get off the fence, so I asked, "Why not a mass migration of Southern whites and leave the Negroes down in their homes? Be easier; there's less whites."

Steve said that was nonsense and Hank and his wife weren't sure if I was pulling their leg. Kay laughed and winked at me. Barbara noticed it, bit her lip.

They batted it around again, off on another tack—that the white race was a minority in the world—and then the conversation died, or maybe they were just tired. Hank's wife jumped up—she had a cute figure standing—and said, "Damn, it's eleven. Our baby sitter is a high school kid and can't stay up late." She nudged Hank with her toe. "Come on, hack, you said you were going to work tonight. Honest, I don't know how he does it, but he'll work till early in the morning."

Steve made his big eyes as he said, "Perhaps the early-morning hours put him in an eerie mood. Someday I'd like to try a TV play of your last mystery. Have to water the sex, but I liked the plot gimmick."

Hank got up and shook himself, belched, rubbed his belly and said, "Those damn potatoes. Try it soon, Stevie, I can use the money. I'm working on one now that ought to go over on TV. Deals with the numbers racket." He looked at me, as if I was Mr. Digit himself.

Barbara said, "Touie should be a gold mine of information for you, Hank; he's a detective."

The silence was like a fog in the room, everybody staring at me with renewed interest, except Kay, who sent a furious glance at Barbara.

"Well, the black eye!" Steve said, popping his eyes. "No offense, old man."

"Say, are you a cop?" Hank asked.

"No. I—eh—well, I work in the post office but do some guard work on the side. Bouncer at dances, stuff like that."

"Yes," Kay put in quickly, "Touie used to be a football player."

Steve yawned. "Maybe we ought to have lunch someday. I'm working on a factual crime series."

"Only a matter of picking up an extra buck for me. Tell you the truth, I haven't worked at it in months," I said, hoping I was lying smoothly.

While Kay got their coats, Hank and his wife had one for the road. I took a shot of straight rum and Steve lit a cigar and walked around the room. Up close, he looked older than I first thought. His teeth were brownish and there were tired lines around his eyes. He could easily have been forty.

When Hank and his wife left, I moved over to the couch and Kay sat beside me. Barbara changed records on the hi-fi. Steve paced the room, puffing on his cigar nervously. He said, "Hank's suspense stories are lousy. He's too too precious for himself. Truman Capote with a gun."*

There was an abrupt change in the atmosphere. Kay said, "This criticism comes to us live, from never-never land. Or is this just some Steve McDonald fill?"

---

* This is *not* a reference to Capote's classic true-crime work, *In Cold Blood*, which was not published until 1966. By 1957, however, Capote had already achieved a reputation as a fine writer of Southern Gothic, with his 1948 novel *Other Voices, Other Rooms* and many short stories and novellas.

Steve blew cigar smoke at her. "Don't waste your small talent; nobody is listening to the audition."

"I think his books have a very subtle and skillful action movement," Kay said, thumbing her nose at Steve. "You're jealous because he's in print."

"Balls with print. Right after the war, when I wrote my guts into my novel, I thought I was made. Damn thing got fine reviews—and never even sold the lousy five hundred advance I received. Hell, any TV show reaches a million times as many people. I must let you have a copy of the book someday, Kay."

"I read it," Barbara said. "It was forced, shallow."

Steve threw his cigar into the fireplace. "What can a high school teacher possibly know about literature? I've had a rough day; let's us all catch the hot combo they have at the Steam Room."

"Wonderful," Kay said. "I'd like a few more belts."

"Why go out? We have plenty to drink here," Barbara put in.

"More fun getting conked* in a night club. Come on, Touie."

"I have to be up early," I began, wondering what the devil she'd meant by conked.

"Don't we all? We'll take in the midnight show and leave. Coming, Bobby?"

Barbara, who seemed to also be Bobby, said in a weary voice, "Oh…all right."

Kay tossed a mink cape over her shoulders as if it were an old shawl while Barbara slipped into a plain fitted cloth coat and a beret. They painted their lips, then bit into tissues to remove the excess lipstick. When they dropped the tissues on a table,

---

* "Conked" usually means to pass out or fall asleep. Lacy uses it here to suggest extreme intoxication, to the point of passing out. Touie reacts to the word because it also refers to a method for straightening hair.

Steve picked them up, said, "Like red Rorschach tests. God, I hate sloppy females." He threw the tissues into the fire.

As I was getting into my overcoat, Barbara took Kay aside, whispered something in her ear. I heard Kay say, "Don't be silly. And so damn touchy!" She was angry, almost slammed her pipe on the table. I felt real lousy—knew damn well what Barbara was "touchy" about. She didn't want to be seen in public with me.

The elevator was so small we had to make two trips. Kay squeezed in with me. She was wearing a faint perfume but I was too mad to pay it any mind. She smiled up at me, her fingers playing with my arm. I said, "Barbara sure cut a hog...with that detective crack."

"She's in one of her moods. But you handled it beautifully." Her fingers stroked my biceps. "Muscles fascinate me."

"What did you mean by getting 'conked'?"

"Conked? Oh, drunk, looped....What did you think I meant?"

"I was just curious." We stepped out into the tiny lobby to wait for Steve and Barbara. An elderly couple came in, gave us both that *look* as they waited for the elevator.

Kay played with my arm again, whispered, "How do you keep in shape?"

"At the Y. Stop feeling me like I was a horse." I nearly said stud horse.

"Don't you like it?"

"I don't mix business and pleasure, to coin a shiny cliché."

"Are you working now?"

"Let's not complicate an employer-employee relationship." I flashed my white teeth as though joking it up, wondering how I could politely tell her I didn't especially want to sleep with her.

Steve and Barbara joined us. As we hailed a cab, Kay asked

where the Jag was and that started a car discussion until we reached the Steam Room. From the outside it seemed to be a large store with a fogged window. I had that tight nervous feeling as we entered, but it fell apart soon as I saw the colored band, and a Negro couple at a table. Checking our coats I looked the place over. It was low ceilinged with cartoon murals on the walls, the lights dim, and the combo beating out a quiet jazz. I'd been to Birdland, Café Society, and some of the "posh" spots, as Sybil called them, in and out of Harlem. But this really had an intimate air, like a movie night spot. The tables surrounding the small dance floor weren't jammed together, and nobody stared at us as we were given one near the bandstand.

When the waiter handed us menus, I was the only one to glance at it. There wasn't any cover or minimum, but at three bucks a shot they didn't need one. They ordered gin and tonic; I took Irish whiskey neat. The girls decided they had to go to the ladies' room and Steve said, "Never saw it to fail; second a woman gets anyplace she has to leak."

"I'll have library send you a biology book tomorrow," Kay told him, walking away.

We listened to the music for a while. It was very smooth, like the old Nat King Cole combo. Steve slipped me a line about writing *the* jazz novel someday. I wanted to tell him he could find material for a book in what a brown musician runs up against on a one-night-stands tour of the South, but didn't. We sipped our drinks and watched a babe putting her "all" into her dancing. "My Lord, what a Diesel motor that bimbo has," Steve said. "How do you like going stag?"

"Stag?"

He flashed his eyes as he smirked, "Man, I see you haven't known Kay long. She and Barbara—Lesbians for years," he added, like a kid mouthing a dirty joke. "Didn't you see them arguing before we left? Bobby didn't want Kay to take her pipe."

I laughed—at myself. Shrugged as I told him, "Democratic country, everybody to their own tastes."

He rubbed his nose with a slim finger. "You're so right. Thanks for bringing me up short. Did you really play much football?" he asked, changing the subject.

The girls returned and I told myself Steve was kidding; they both looked very feminine. Kay asked, "Dance?"

I stood up. "Okay, but I'm not much of a dancer."

I took her in my arms and we glided around smoothly enough to pass for dancing. She said, "Sorry to leave you alone with Steve."

"What's he got, the measles?"

"Oh Lord! Can't you tell, Touie? He's as queer as a six-bit coin. What are you grinning about?"

"Your hair is tickling my chin."

"By radar? I'm inches from you," she said, putting her head on my shoulder. "Do you like this place?"

"Aha."

"I trust you'll pad it into your swindle sheet."*

"Don't worry about it."

After another round of drinks I danced with Barbara and noticed she was wearing a wedding ring like Kay's. She gave me a workout, although Steve was on the floor with Kay and Barbara kept following them with her eyes. He was a good dancer. When she saw me watching her she smiled up at me, said, "Sorry. But I can't stand that smug creature. Because he finally has a TV show, he acts as if he had the world by the tail. And the boyish act: the crew cut and the college clothes—the

---

* Slang for an expense account.

ass. I don't know why Kay lets him hang around. Ever have the misfortune to read his book?"

"Nope."

"Trash. Naturalism at its worst." She rubbed her gray head on my tie. "How tall are you?"

"About six-two."

So she told me what an athlete she'd been in college; talked until we sat down. Steve was wiping his face with a napkin, said, "This is actually becoming a steam room. Are you a Turkish bath *aficionado*, Touie?"

"Never in one."

"No, I suppose not," he said, motioning for the waiter. Instead of a drink I ordered a club sandwich. The show came on. The "show" was a tall girl with a faraway look on a powdered death-mask face, her eyebrows painted in like two darts. She sang a torch song—off key. After the second song it got to me, or maybe I was getting a little high.

The sandwich was dressed in pants* and had a crazy border of pickle chips and olives. It impressed me, seemed the most high-class sandwich I'd ever had. I paid more attention to it than to Kay's knee wearing my trouser thin.

I ate slowly, listening to the weird singing, glanced around the table. I couldn't fully make any of them: they were all a little phony. So was the Steam Room. Yet I'd long lost the blue mood Sybil had put me in. I'd forgotten the dumb fight in the coffeepot, even about blowing the whistle on Thomas. This was big time. I had to admit that, phony or not, I liked it.

It wasn't even much of a shock to admit I liked playing the pet Negro...well, at least a little.

---

* Touie presumably means that the sandwich was partially wrapped in paper.

TWO DAYS
AGO

4

I was between the sheets before two—my own sheets. I'd insisted upon splitting the thirty-one-dollar tab with Steve, although Kay had whispered, "Let him take it, he comes from a loaded family." We'd taken the girls home, then I dropped Steve off at Sixty-fifth Street and taxied all the way uptown like a big shot.

At six the alarm dragged me out of a deep sleep. Dressing quickly in slacks and an old sweat shirt, I was parked on Thomas' block when he came out at 7:35 A.M. I followed him to Twenty-third Street, where he stopped for breakfast, and at 8:21 A.M. I watched him enter the freight-company building, whistling cheerfully.

I drove home, lucked up on a parking space. I had a glass of milk, picked up a new *Jet* Ollie had brought in, and hit the sack, reading myself to sleep.

I awoke after one, came awake and hungry under a shower. Sybil phoned as I was dressing; I'd forgotten it was her day off. She horsed around about wanting me to drive her to a beauty parlor on 126th Street, to have her hair touched up, and finally asked what she really wanted to say—had I decided to take the

P.O. job? I said I still had time to make up my mind and at the moment only food was on my brain. She said she was making lunch. I drove over to her place, decided not to say anything about last night.

Sybil looked all rested and pretty, sort of springy. Her lips were a very lush red. I wanted to kiss her but let it alone. I was still annoyed by her putting things on a my-becoming-a-postman-or-else basis. But I was feeling too good for an argument. When I drove her to 126th Street I had a couple of hours to kill, considered taking a swim at the Y, then decided I might as well do some work for Ted Bailey.

His letter said the James woman was fifty-two years old, had worked in a hospital, and her last address was a crummy rooming house on 131st Street. There was a set of penciled instructions pasted next to the bell outside this ancient private house: ring one for Flatts, two for Adams, and a Stewart—probably on the top floor—got a serenade of ten bells. Of course there wasn't any James listed, but some of the names were so faded you couldn't make them out.

I went down to the basement and rang. A teen-age chick, wearing overbright lipstick, narrow dungarees, a club sweater and a plaid men's shirt that didn't hide her pointed breasts, answered the door. She was chewing gum and very sure of her young figure and cute face—no one could tell her she wasn't the sharpest chick this side of nothing. I figured Mrs. James hadn't moved, merely arranged with her landlady to give the bill collector the runaround. She'd changed jobs, but a person with a combination stove-refrigerator doesn't flit from room to room.

When I asked for Mrs. James the girl showed me how well she could snap her gum as she asked, "Who you?"

"Friend of hers, in town for the day."

"Friend, she moved out last month."

"Do you know where? I haven't got much time and I'd like to see her."

She shrugged, both of us watching what danced. "Naw. I think out on Long Island someplace."

She wasn't much of a liar. "Too bad. I have some money for her. Phoned the hospital but they told me she left. Now I can't mail it to her either. Well, maybe I'll run into her one of these days."

Miss Fine Brown Frame gave me a practiced look through her long eyelashes. "What town did you say you came from, big boy?"

"Drove in from Chicago. Her cousin lives there."

"Well..." The bright eyes ran over me slowly, decided my clothes looked like money. "Tell you a secret, she does live here. Five bells. But she won't be home till four. She's ducking one of them damn credit companies, that's why I gave you a bum steer before. You either come back here, or call her at the Boulevard Hospital—that's over in the Bronx—tonight. She started working there last week."

"Thanks. And, honey, they sure grow some fine young stuff around here."

She snapped her gum with obvious pleasure. "Yeah man, but they don't grow no corn. This is the Big Apple, buster." She shut the door with a little curtsy. Kids today; everything for effect.

I drove along 125th Street, found an empty space, dropped a dime in the meter. One-twenty-fifth is something like a small-town main street; wait long enough and you must see somebody you know. I'd hardly got my pipe going when two clowns rushed over to the Jag, said, "Touie! How's every little thing?"

"I'm just here," I said, shaking hands, wondering who they were. Turned out we'd been in the army together. I left the Jag and took them into Frank's, bought beers, and made a lot of small talk about that magic land—old times. I left after the second beer, drove back to 131st Street, pressed the bell five times.

A small but spry-looking coffee-brown woman opened the door a moment later. Her face was old and her hands work-worn, but her eyes were young and she had an excited way of talking, gushing like an eager young thing. When I asked, "Mrs. James?" she said, "You must be the Chicago man Esther said was just here, my cousin Jane's friend. How is she? I keep meaning to write her but...Excuse me, step inside."

The narrow hallway was in need of paint, a thready carpet ran up the wooden steps—a firetrap. We seemed to be alone and I said, "I don't know your cousin, Mrs. James," and flashed my badge. "Ducking payment on that stove-refrigerator is the same thing as stealing."

She seemed to age in a split second, to shrivel up as she fell against the wall—as if I'd socked her in the stomach. Her face was a sickly brown, and then her eyes got angry and she pulled herself together, was really boiling. "Why you goddam lousy ass-licker! The 'man' downtown can always manage to find one of our folks to be a Judas! I never—"

"Cut that talk," I snapped, both of us keeping our voices low, hers a hiss.

"Why?" she asked, sticking her thin face forward. "Why should I keep still? You going to hit me? Try it; I'll be the *last* brown woman you ever lay a hand on!"

"Mrs. James, take it easy. I'm only doing my job. Stop all the big talk about the 'man' and anybody threatening you. If you ran a store and somebody tried a skip on you, you'd be the first to raise the roof. Listen to me, you're a decent, hard-working woman, and I know you wouldn't think of stealing, but—"

"Stealing? That damn company is the crook! I paid $320 for that kitchen combination, plus interest and handling charges.

Fifty dollars down and twenty a month. Now you listen to me! A month—one month, mind you—after I bought the combination I see the exact same thing in Macy's for $140! What do you think of that? I go down to the company and damn if they ain't selling it for $260 themselves. Well, I made up my mind I work too hard for my money to give it away. I've paid them $150, plus their lousy charges, and that's all they're going to get!"

"Mrs. James, why do you get involved in these installment deals? It's always cheaper to buy anything outright from a big store."

"You talk like you have a paper head! Where am I ever going to get $140 all at one time? I *got* to buy on installment. You think I have anything to spare on that little salary they pay me at the hospital? Talk sense, boy!"

I felt both lousy and angry—mad at her. Most of these installment joints make their money playing the poor for suckers. I was sore at her for being so dumb; she probably could have gone to a big department store and still bought the damn thing on time. But somehow it always turns out that the people who can afford to pay the least end up paying the most. Still, that wasn't my business. I said, "Look, Mrs. James, let's both of us talk some sense. You don't have to tell me how hard you work, that you're probably overpaying for your room, your food, and everything else. But nobody twisted your arm to make you buy this kitchen combination. Sure, you made a bad deal, but you're a grown woman and you signed a contract. I don't have to tell you the law is on their side. They can come up today and yank the combination out and you haven't a legal peep. It's a mess, but you got yourself into it with your eyes open. Now, you'd better decide what you're going to do—lose everything or get up to date on your payments." The words had a rotten taste as I mouthed them.

She began to weep, hard tiny tears. "A person tries to live decent, get a little joy out of life and—"

"A punk sticking somebody up with a gun can say the same thing."

"I'm not a crook! Don't you dare call me that. I never did a dishonest thing in my life! You…you…big *black bastard*!" Her wet eyes were glaring fiercely at me as she said, "There, I never called anybody that before—may God cut out my tongue—but I say it to you, you with a skin as dark as mine!"

I couldn't have felt worse if she'd spit in my face. I mumbled, "Lady, I'm only doing my job, a routine—"

"Job? Is it your job to torture and help swindle your own people? 'Man' downtown gets the pie and you croak about a job and take the crumbs. All right, tell 'em I'll send a money order tomorrow, get up on my payments. Now get out of my sight!"

"How much do you still owe?"

"About $170. Get out of here, I said I'll pay."

"How much can you pay today?"

"What you want, my blood?"

"Goddamnit, stop the dramatics! I'm trying to help you. Maybe I can get them to make a settlement."

"Well, even though I didn't intend to pay, I've been saving the payment money. I suppose I could give them a hundred dollars by the end of the week."

"Is there a phone here?"

She nodded down the hall. There was a pay phone behind the steps. I phoned Bailey, told him, "Ted, I'm with Mrs. James. She's strictly a deadbeat. Ill and out of a job. I doubt if she'll be able to work for months. She owes $170 but thinks she can borrow $100 from a friend, if they'll settle. Otherwise, you'll have to take the combination back, and it's in rough shape. The hundred is all the dough she has in the world, all she can raise. I'd advise taking it. She can bring it down in a day or two."

Ted said he'd check and phone me back. I told him to make it fast, to remind the company they'd already made a profit on the deal, that the combination was now selling for half of what they had charged her.

I lit my pipe and waited in the narrow hallway, neither of us talking. Mrs. James stared at me with sullen eyes, hating my guts, my good clothes. It was four seventeen. Fooling around with this two-bit case would make me miss Thomas.

Ted called back, said it was okay. He wanted to speak to the old lady and she told him she'd have the money in the mail by the end of the week. "Yes, yes. I understand. Positively. Yes!"

When she hung up, slamming the receiver down, I said, "Now, Mrs. James, when you pay make certain to get a receipt saying 'paid in full.' Or if you mail in the money, get a check from a bank and write on the back of it, 'Final and full payment for kitchen combination, as per agreement.' Next time you buy anything on time, think what you're doing first, and don't start whining afterward."

"You, get out! You've done your 'job.'"

"I went out on a limb for you, saved you seventy bucks, Mrs. James."

"You waiting for a tip?"

"Of course not, but at least, well…I did my best for you. I mean, I understand the spot you're in, we're all in."

"Thank you. Thanks for nothing!"

I shrugged, put on my hat, and headed for the door. She stood at the foot of the steps, still looking at me as if I were something a dog had dropped. I walked out, slamming the door hard, drove downtown. Traffic was heavy and it was after five when I reached the freight company. Cursing, I drove toward

Brooklyn and the welding school, changed my mind, double-parked in front of the cafeteria on Twenty-third Street. Thomas was inside having supper, his bus-girl friend hovering around his table, both of them laughing and wisecracking.

I felt a little better until a cop came over and asked what I was doing. He was an old cop, with a red-veined white face and a lousy set of false teeth. When he talked just the lower part of his mouth moved. I told him I was waiting for a friend and he said I couldn't double-park on Twenty-third Street, didn't I know that? I said I was sorry and started the Jaguar and he asked for my license. If he had a cellophane head I couldn't have seen his little bird brain working any clearer: a colored man in an expensive car—S.O.P.—it must be a stolen heap. I showed him my license and registration, praying Thomas didn't look out the window and see me.

The cop grunted, "I'll give you a ticket the next time I catch you double-parking," as he handed my license back.

"I don't doubt that you will."

"Get fresh and I'll give you a ticket right now!"

"Who's 'fresh'? You said something and I answered you," I said, crawling slightly, all the anger I'd felt at Mrs. James welling up in me.

He took out his notebook, muttered, "I'll just take down your name and license number, smart guy. Be sure I remember it." His lower lip was moving like a ventriloquist's dummy.

I shut up; no point in talking myself into a ticket. When he finished scribbling I asked, "Can I go now?"

Another grunt: "Yeah."

I found a parking space over on Ninth Avenue and walked back to take a plant across the street from the cafeteria, telling myself I was a dummy to talk to the cop; if he saw me now it might start another verbal fight.

Thomas took his time eating and I was getting hungry myself. Finally he and Miss Burns checked their watches and he walked out and up to his room. I stopped at the corner, where I could keep an eye on his house without being conspicuous. He came out at seven, wearing a shirt and tie under his windbreaker, his blond hair carefully brushed. He picked up his girl in front of the cafeteria and they went across the street and into a movie.

I phoned Kay but Barbara said she wasn't in and I left a message that everything was under control. Bobby didn't ask any questions. I phoned Sybil to ask if she wanted to eat Chinese food. She said she'd already eaten but would have supper waiting for me, and to bring in some beer.

After circling Sybil's place several times in ever larger circles, I found a parking space, brought in a couple bottles of High Life. Sybil gave me a plate of reheated stew with gummy rice, garlic bread, and salad. She had her hair up in curlers, which I hate, but otherwise she was in a good mood, didn't even mention the P.O. once. I kept thinking about Mrs. James and I told Sybil about it and she said, "What can you expect from poor-ass Negroes?" Only she didn't say Negroes and I got boiling and she sat on my lap, kissing me slowly and asking between each kiss, "What's the matter with my big Touie?"

Of course it was corny as the devil, but it worked. I looked at Sybil's pretty face, my hands playing with her good body, and I thought about the TV job and wondered what I had to be angry about.

After I washed the dishes we drank the beer and watched TV, then played gin while waiting for the fights to come on. About eleven, right after the news, as we were settling down to watch a late movie, an English one, the phone rang. Sybil said it was for me. Ollie said, "Knew where to find you, old man. Look, you just got a phone call from a woman named Miss

Robbens. She said it was very important I reach you at once. I told her I could find you and she said to give you this message: you're to meet her in Tutt's room, inside the room, at exactly midnight."

"*In* the room? Ollie, sure you have that straight, *inside* the room?"

"You too? I'm going to resign as your private secretary. Look, I wrote the message down and she even had me repeat it over the phone. She sounded excited, kept asking if I could reach you for sure. I told her not to worry, I'd carry it to you. Got it, sleuth? Exactly midnight in Tutt's room. Doesn't give you much time."

"Yes. You're certain I'm to go into the room?"

Ollie sighed. "Told you I wrote it down, repeated it back to her. I'm reading it now. You straight, old man?"

"Yeah. Yeah. Thanks, Ollie."

I hung up and dialed Kay. Barbara answered, sounding half asleep. She told me Kay was out, that she hadn't seen her since morning. Then she suddenly asked, with new life in her voice, "Touie, haven't you seen Kay tonight?"

I said no and hung up. As I put on my tie and shoes, Sybil asked, "What's up?"

"I don't know."

"You look worried."

"I sure am. Something's happened on this Madison Avenue TV deal, something I don't understand." I kept thinking that if Kay wanted me to meet her in Thomas' room, the secret must be out and the whole damn publicity deal off—and I was off the case too.

"If you were in the P.O., you wouldn't have to go chasing off in the middle of the night or—"

"Not now, honey," I said, kissing her good night. "Maybe I'll be back."

"No you don't, don't you break into my sleep—I have to make time tomorrow. I'm going shopping before I go into work."

"Then I'll phone you on the job, as usual."

It was eleven eighteen when I started for my car, then hailed a cab on Broadway. I wouldn't have time to play hide and seek with a parking space downtown. I got out my notebook— Thomas-Tutt had room 3 in apartment 2F. Damn, if I was off the case I'd have to give back part of the retainer and I had less than fifty bucks on me. Although Kay had said a minimum of a month. Of course I didn't have to give back a dime, legally, but I wanted to retain Kay's good will. If there was a snafu, why call me to his room? Kay could phone me the deal was off and that would be that. Or did going to his room mean I was still working? Or...

I sat up straight as the cowboy at the wheel cut into the highway on two wheels. This could only mean one thing—Thomas had taken a powder! Sure, Kay had found out—somehow— he'd flown the coop, and I was up the creek. Me and my big detective agency, couldn't even handle a simple shadow job. But hell, she'd told me herself I only had to check on him twice a day until his case was televised. He was taking his girl to the movies a few hours ago, unless he was smarter than he looked, Thomas wasn't getting ready to run. And how would Kay know? Or was she having somebody else check on Thomas too? And on me?

I paid the cabbie off on the corner. It was still seven minutes before midnight. The house and the block were quiet. I stood in front of the house for a moment. Why *exactly* at midnight? Two middle-aged stinking winos came out of the house, gave me the usual *look,* but with bleary-eyed trimmings. As I went up the few steps to the doorway, they wobbled down the street, glancing back at me and mumbling something.

I stood outside 2F, a dim and crummy hallway smelling

of stale food and various human stinks. Harlem didn't have a monopoly on lousy houses. I tried the doorknob; it wasn't locked. Another hallway, narrower, hotter, with rooms opening off it. There was a dirty metal "3" on the door nearest the main door. I listened and didn't hear a thing, but there was light coming through the crack under the door. I rapped gently, waited a few seconds, turned the knob and the door opened.

I suppose as soon as I saw the messed-up room I knew the score. Only I couldn't quite believe it.

It was a small room, with only a bed and a metal dresser—all the drawers out and ransacked. Thomas seemed to be sleeping in bed, covers pulled up over his head. I had a sudden, sickening hunch the person in bed might be Kay. Closing the door, I stepped over Thomas' pants and windbreaker on the floor, and then I saw the wet blood on the gray pillow. There was a large pair of bloody pliers on the floor.

Pulling back the covers I saw the back of Thomas' head bashed in. He was face down, blood all over his head and shoulders, blood still wet. It was even splattered on the cheap-pink painted wall behind the bed.

I stood there like a dummy, still holding the cover with my fingertips, knowing I had to think damn fast, and afraid of what I was thinking. I didn't have to be a detective to know what all this meant.

Maybe I stood there a few seconds, even a few minutes. There were footsteps on the stairs, at the outside door. In the back of my mind, the only part that was thinking clearly, I expected them. I dropped the blanket as the door flew open—a thick-faced white cop stood there. He wasn't expecting a body but when he saw the bloody bed his gun flew out of his heavy blue overcoat pocket like his hand was on springs. His deep voice said, "Keep your hands in sight, up, you black sonofabitch! Got you dead to rights." Maybe it was my imagination but I thought he sounded almost happy—thinking of a promotion.

What I'd known since I first got Ollie's call came into sharp focus: I'd been had, been set up for this from the go. Now my mind was clear and racing—the cops would learn about the fight in the coffeepot when they checked at the school, the beat cop in Brooklyn would remember me, so would the fat cop who wanted to give me a ticket at suppertime. And the winos seeing me enter the house a few minutes ago. I'd been had but tight.

I held my hands up, shoulder high. The cop was alone, probably the beat cop. *Exactly at midnight.* The timing was so simple, a phone call to the precinct at five to midnight saying there was trouble in room 3, apartment 2F, and the post cop catching me. I was cold cocked.

He was staring at me, waiting for me to say something. I didn't bother making words. It boiled down to a white cop and black me, and he had the "difference" in his hand. I'd look silly trying to explain…all I could do was stand very still.

In that split second something my old man used to say rushed through my mind. *"A Negro's life is dirt cheap because he hasn't any rights a white man must respect. That's the law, the Dred Scott Decision, son.** *Always remember that."*

I was remembering; any move on my part and I'd be dead.

"Why don't you robbing bastards stay up in Harlem where

---

* *Dred Scott v. Sandford* was decided in 1857 by the US Supreme Court. The enslaved Scott sued to declare that by reason of his having traveled with his owner from Missouri (a slave state) to Illinois (a free state) and then to the Wisconsin Territory (also free), he was free. The Supreme Court held Scott had no standing to sue on the grounds that Black people could not be US citizens. The court did not stop there, however, also finding that the Missouri Compromise, legislation intended to assuage the growing conflict over slavery among the states, was unconstitutional. Scholars have called the ruling the worst decision ever entered by the Supreme Court for its racism, flawed logic, distorted historical basis, and convoluted reading of the Constitution. At the time, it was viewed as a victory for Southern forces, galvanizing the antislavery movement and fueling the Civil War.

you belong instead of coming down here to rob and mug people?" His voice was shrill, his white face working with rage as he stepped toward me.

Within striking distance, he raised his gun to whip my head. The second the gun was out of line with my face, with reflex action, my left shot out and grabbed his gun hand by the wrist. My right knee thudded into his groin and my right hand clubbed him on the side of the jaw.

He didn't have a chance to fire at the ceiling; he crumpled in a heap on the floor, moaning, his heavy mouth open wide, fighting for air. I stepped over him, closed the door, walked down the stairs as fast and quietly as I could.

ONE DAY
AGO

5

The street was empty.

I tried to hold my shaking legs from running as I walked toward Seventh Avenue. A store-window clock said it was nine minutes past midnight. I walked up a block, stopped a cab, told him to take me to Grand Central Station.

It was neat—I'd been framed like a picture. Wasn't only the murder troubling me. In the eyes of the police I'd committed a greater crime than murder—I'd slugged a cop. They'd beat me crazy in the station house before I was even arraigned on the murder rap. It was all so pat, not even a tiny loophole. I didn't have the faintest smell of an alibi. Judging by the wetness of the blood, Thomas had been killed ten or fifteen minutes before I got there. It all had been set, to the smallest detail. I was finished. I was dead. With the cop-slugging over my head, I was worse than dead.

The hell of it was I knew the killer, but that didn't help me. Of course it had to be Kay. Everything added: picking a colored detective, knowing I'd stand out; the hush-hush bunk, paying me out of "petty cash"—I couldn't even prove I was working for her. But what did Kay have against Thomas? Or was the whole TV pitch a lie?

As I paid the cabbie at Grand Central I put on an act, saying I hoped I could still catch the New Haven train. The police would be checking all cabs soon.

I walked through the station, then down Lexington to Kay's house. I was real mixed up. Somehow I couldn't picture Kay killing him like that, not bashing his head with the pliers. I could see her using a gun but not getting close enough to bust his head. That didn't figure, but everything else added to Kay. I was taking a big chance seeing her. I could be walking into a room full of cops: she'd certainly be expecting me, have a trap ready. But I could hardly be in a tighter squeeze than I was now and I *had* to see her, confront her. It was my only hope: these perfect-crime jokers sometimes plan too carefully, trip themselves.

I stood on the corner, didn't see a soul around her house. I walked down the block fast, ducked into her doorway. I couldn't risk ringing a bell to open the door. It was an old door. Holding the knob with one hand I leaned back and hit the door just under the lock with a hip block. It jumped open with a dull sound that was magnified by the stillness. I waited; the ground-floor apartment doors didn't open. I stepped in. The lock wasn't too badly sprung—I managed to close the door. I rode the midget elevator to Kay's apartment, rang the bell.

There wasn't a sound. I rang again, long and loud. There was the padding sound of slippered feet approaching the door; Barbara asked, "Who is it?"

"Touie."

"Who? Oh....It's late," she said, opening the door.

I pushed by her, closed the door. She was wearing a kind of thin red ski pajamas and she looked tired, maybe a little drunk. I walked and pushed her into the nearest chair, told her, "Sit still for a second." I ran through the apartment, keeping the doors open to see if she went for the phone.

Bobby was alone.

When I returned to the living room she was fumbling at lighting a cigarette, her hand shaking badly. "What's all this about?"

"Where's Kay?" I asked standing over her.

"I wish I knew. No, I wish I didn't know."

I grabbed her thin shoulders, shook her. "Don't play it cute. Where is she?"

Bobby pulled herself together, tried to push my hands away as she asked, "By what right do you place your hands on me?"

Under other circumstances it would have been for laughs. I shook her again. "Damnit, sober up. I'm in a jam. Where's Kay?"

"I took sleeping pills some time ago; my head isn't very clear. Really, I don't know where Kay is. What's your trouble, Toussaint? Oh, that's a beautiful name. I wish I had a name like—"

"A man's been murdered and the police are looking for me. Does that get through to you? Murder! Kay framed me, set me up for this rap."

Bobby's eyes seemed to brighten, become almost normal. "Kay? Oh my no. Kay can be silly and mean, but never vicious. Really, a murder?"

"Yes, goddamnit, *really*!"

"Who?" Her eyes went wide and she tried to stand as she said, "Not Kay!" and her voice rose to a scream.

I pushed her back into the chair. "Cut it out, and wake up. The guy Kay hired me to watch, he's been killed. How much do you know about this TV stuff?"

"All of it. Sorry I nearly ruined everything last night. Kay bawled me out as if—"

"Bobby, listen to me, I don't have time for small talk. I don't have time for anything. Where's Kay?"

"With a so-called man."

"Who? Her husband?"

She gave me a long look, then threw her head back and laughed hysterically. I shook her hard and she said, "She's with that pansy writer Steve. I'm her husband." She added this last with quiet dignity in her voice. Her eyes were proud as she stared up at me and said soberly, "Yes, I'm what is known as the Butch* in our setup. Now what's all this nonsense about Kay framing you?"

"She left a call at my office for me to go to Thomas' room at midnight. I found him murdered; a moment later a cop came busting in. It all fits; the reason Kay lured me, knowing a Negro would be easy to spot, a setup for this frame. But I'm going to find Kay, get the truth out of her if it's the—"

"Are you saying Kay killed this man?" Bobby cut in, crushing her cigarette on the glass table top.

"You say it, say it any way you want."

"That's ridiculous. And Kay didn't pick you for this job, I did."

"You? Don't cover for her. Bobby, I don't want to get rough but this isn't the time for stalling!"

"I'm not stalling. I'm telling you the truth. I met your friend Sid at a party and somehow he mentioned you. Kay had told me about this publicity stunt of hers, about hiring a detective. She was looking forward to it…and…I knew she was restless. I've seen it happen before. She goes off with a…a…man. Of course she's always come running back to me after a night or two, but I live in a nightmare that she won't return. Can you understand how much I love that girl?"

---

* Note that Kay, who never states that she is queer, used this nickname for her "husband," whom we soon learn was Barbara. Originally, earlier in the twentieth century, "butch" meant overtly masculine, but by the 1950s, it took on the meaning of the more "masculine" partner in a lesbian duo. We'll see that like many men of the 1950s, Toussaint has nothing particularly negative to say about a relationship between two women, but he asks pointedly whether Tutt is a "pansy" or "queer."

"Skip the love story. Why did you pick me?"

"No, you can't understand what Kay means to me. I simply told her about you, knowing full well she'd like the idea of...I mean, of you being a Negro. I was so pleased when I saw you last night, all your muscles, your...manliness. You were perfect for the affair."

"Affair? What the devil are you talking about?"

"My dear Toussaint—that exciting name—isn't it obvious? Any relationship between Kay and you could only be temporary, hardly permanent....You're a Negro."

"For—! I've had enough of this crap, where's Kay now?"

"Wherever she is, it's your fault. She was disgusting, pawing you last night, but you didn't react. Now she's spending the night in some hotel with that horrid creature Steve. That's what worries me. Kay usually goes for the brute type."

"What hotel?"

"I'm sure I don't know."

I shook her again. "Damn you, this isn't a game! What hotel?"

The crazy thing was, her breasts danced as I shook her and yet a hard voice, almost a man's voice, barked, "Get your damn hands off me! I told you I don't know. If I knew, do you imagine I'd be sitting here? I'd go up and drag her back home!"

I walked around the living room, thinking hard. If what Bobby said was true, and I had this feeling it was, then it knocked the props out on my Kay-framing-me idea. But if it wasn't Kay, who did frame me and why? Who could possibly have known about my tailing Thomas? Supposed to be all top secret, just Kay and her boss—and Barbara. "What's the name of Kay's boss?"

"I don't know, Brooks somethingorother. Kay calls him B.H." She shook her head. "Forget about him; he's been out in St. Louis opening a new station for Central. Kay mentioned he had phoned her from there this afternoon."

"You said you hadn't seen Kay since yesterday morning."

"She phoned me at school, during lunch hour, to—to tell me she was leaving me." Bobby began to weep.

I stood there, listening, for some stupid reason, to her crying. It didn't sound phony. Things had been simple when I came up here: I was a dead duck with one possible out—find Kay and get the truth from her, beat it out of her if necessary. Now...? I didn't rule Kay off the list, not till I knew where she'd been when Thomas was killed. But I'd been certain she'd framed me from the go, and that wasn't so. Now...? Now I realized the only way to save my neck was to find the killer before the police found me. I was mixed up: somehow relieved and even encouraged by knowing Kay hadn't double-crossed me, and a little frightened that I was on my own. I really wasn't a detective but a strong-arm bouncer, a slob good at scaring women like Mrs. James. And no one but me, a half-ass detective, could save my life!

I began pacing the room again, trying to think logically. From the little I'd seen of Tutt-Thomas he appeared to be a hard-working joker, living down his past. That didn't rule out the possibility he was in a jam here, but it was unlikely....He had a record, would be careful. If he was doing anything shady here, why would he be sweating at the freight company, going to a trade school? Hell, he hardly had enough free time to get in trouble. He was strictly small time, a home-town hood-lum....Only one thing would make sense: some old buddy had knocked him off for revenge. But how did I fit into that picture? And if it was an old buddy, why wait all these years? Perhaps he'd just located Thomas, or maybe been released from a pen a couple days ago, went gunning for Thomas. But how would he—or she—know about me, about Kay? Of course Kay said they'd already interviewed people in Thomas' home town.... Sure, this joker had been hunting for Thomas for years, and the TV idea gives him his lead. Suppose he was tailing Kay *and* Thomas? That made hard sense. Unknowingly Kay had taken him to Thomas and to me; from that point it wouldn't take a genius to set me up for murder.

I felt much better, as if I'd accomplished something. But there was one loose end I had to tie. I said, "It was a horrible sight, Thomas' *bald* head split open, his rooms ransacked."

Bobby didn't say a word, dried her eyes with her sleeve. Okay, I was clumsy, I didn't trip her. I stopped being cute. "When was the last time you saw Thomas?"

"I never saw him. I—" She looked up at me. "Are you crazy, Touie, first accusing Kay and now me?"

"Look, there's only four people knew I was hired to shadow Thomas: Kay, myself, B.H., and you."

"Oh, for goodness' sake, I've been home all night. You know that—you called me early in the evening and again about an hour ago. It was after your second call I took the sleeping pills."

That was good enough for me, even if it wasn't air tight. I couldn't see Bobby having the guts to kill. I waved my hands. "I have to consider all angles. Bobby, Kay, said the TV show had a complete file on Thomas; did she ever tell you any of the details?"

"Vaguely, something about rape. I wasn't too interested in such sordid matters. She has some files in her desk; Kay often works here afternoons, and evenings."

I followed her into the bedroom to an oval-shaped desk of ebony wood at one window. There was a typewriter on top of a small file cabinet next to the desk. She leafed through the cabinet, handed me a fairly thick folder with a neatly typed sticker TUTT-THOMAS pasted on it.

It was a good file, names, dates, interviews, and even a few pictures. I rolled it up, shoved it in my pocket. I felt almost happy; I could really work with this. It meant I'd have to get to his home town, Bingston, Ohio, damn fast. That wasn't a bad idea either; it would be dangerous for me to hang around New York.

"I'm going now. Bobby, can I trust you? Are you going to phone the police as soon as I leave?"

"Certainly not."

"My life is at stake, melodramatic as it may sound. I need time. Do you think you can convince Kay and the TV studio not to say anything about Thomas for a few days?"

"Kay will have to do whatever Central does, but if I know TV and their fear of adverse publicity, they won't make any fuss unless forced to. Toussaint, I'm terribly sorry you're involved in this. I truly don't believe you would kill a person."

"Thanks." We were walking toward the door.

"Is there anything else I can do to help you?"

I wanted to ask her for money but couldn't bring myself to do it. "Barbara, if this gets messy, I mean, if I'm caught, our story is I dropped up here to shoot the breeze, stole this file while you were in the john. That will leave you in the clear. One thing you can do, find Kay and tell her to keep quiet." I added a cover-up: "I'll be hanging around the city, hiding out, so tell Kay not to make any effort to contact me."

At the door she squeezed my hand and began weeping again as she said, "Good luck, Toussaint. May God be with you."

I was jittery riding down the elevator, looking up and down the empty street. Then I suddenly laughed and walked boldly over to Third Avenue, waited for a bus. I was fairly safe. The police would be looking for *a* Negro—but to whites we all look alike, and that was my protection. Except for my size, which fitted the usual "burly" Negro type the papers blame for anything and everything, I wasn't in much danger. Although by this time the cop would have given them a description of my clothes.

On the ride uptown I read through the file carefully, making notes of what sounded important. I decided I couldn't risk going home. I only had thirty-eight dollars on me. I needed money, but I doubted if Ollie would still have the rent dough around I'd left for him. I got off at 149th Street, walked toward the Drive.

I had to ring Sybil's bell four times before she came to the door in a sheer nightgown, asked, "Are you off your head, Touie? It's almost—Why it is three in the morning! I told you I had to be up early...."

"Honey, I'm in a rough jam. I can't tell you about it—it's best you don't know. But I have to leave for Chicago at once and I need money."

"A jam? With that Madison Avenue woman?"

"Honey, don't ask questions. And it hasn't anything to do with her. Sybil, I have to grab a plane at once. How much can you lend me?"

She shook herself awake. "I still have the eighty-five dollars you gave me."

"Any more?"

She went to a drawer and took out her purse; a sleepy, flat-footed walk. "I knew it was too good getting that money from you. Here, I have seven, eight—nine dollars more. That makes ninety-four dollars. When am I going to get this back?"

"Soon. Now honey, if the police come here and   "

Her eyes came wide awake as she cut in with "Police? Touie, what kind of trouble are you in?"

"Don't ask. And for everybody's sake don't say anything about this, talk around. But if the cops do question you, tell them the truth. I borrowed some money and I'm on my way to Chicago and Canada. Now I have to rush. 'Bye, baby."

"But...? That's ninety-four dollars you owe me, Touie Moore."

"Don't worry about it." I blew her a kiss and walked up to where I'd parked the Jag. I drove across the George Washington Bridge, half expecting a road block. I got both tanks full of gas, oil, water, and a bunch of road maps at the first gas station open. I knew it would be easy to spot my Jag, something the attendant would remember. But there wasn't anything I could do about it, except steal a car, or steal different license plates.

But I didn't know how to steal a car. Taking license plates off a parked car would be simple—but it could mean more trouble; if I was stopped for going through a light or anything and had to show my license, I'd be cooked. The best thing was to keep to the Jag. If I got any sort of break, the police wouldn't know Thomas' identity for a day, and wouldn't know about me for a couple of days. By that time I'd be dead if I didn't come up with at least a sure lead. Hell, my money would only last about a week.

At 4:20 A.M. I started cutting across New Jersey toward Pennsylvania and Ohio. I drove carefully, not too fast, and the Jaguar ate up the road in the quiet darkness as I wondered how much longer I'd be able to drive it—or any car. I kept the radio on but the killing didn't make the news. Most of the time I felt confident, although now and then I had this doubt that I wasn't being a detective, I was merely on the run.

In the middle of the morning I stopped again for gas, then turned into a deserted side road and walked around to relax my cramped legs. It was a cold, sunny day, and it felt good to walk on the grass and dirt, fill my lungs with the clean air.

I drove till noon, when I stopped at a small roadside restaurant. There were several trucks parked outside, so I figured the food would be okay. A moon-faced woman with wild white hair was behind the counter, serving the truckers. As I sat on a stool this biddy shrieked, "No you don't! I don't serve no colored here. Don't you see the sign?" She pointed a fat finger at a fly-specked WE RESERVE THE RIGHT TO REFUSE SERVICE... sign.

I was in Pennsylvania and I told her, "That sign is so much cardboard. There's a state civil-rights law here." I wasn't sure if there was or not, and was too tired and rattled to think straight.

"I go by a higher law—God. If God had meant you to be white he would have made us all the same. Now get!"

One of the truck jockeys snickered and I wanted to hit him so badly I thought I'd explode. But a rumble was the very last thing I could chance now. I stood up and told the old bitch, "You sure fooled me. I thought this was a 'colored' place. I mean, seeing you, your face and the hard hair   bet you got as much 'colored' blood in you as I have. That's why I sat down, seeing you."

I walked out hearing her scream, ashamed of myself for such childish stupidity. Still, I had to hit back, some way. One thing was for sure, as the song says, when you leave Manhattan you're not going anyplace.*

As I turned the Jag back toward the road, one of the truckers came out—not the one who'd snickered—said, "Wait a minute, Mac." He walked over to the Jag and I got out fast, knowing I couldn't control myself any longer. He was a little guy, compactly built, freckles on his pale face. He had a thermos under his arm and held it out as he said, "Old Ma hasn't all her buttons. You want some hot java, I have a thermos full you're welcome to."

"Thanks a lot. But I'll get a regular meal some other place. But thanks again."

"Suit yourself. Guess you must be a musician, huh?"

---

* "New York's My Home" by Gordon Jenkins (1946) was first released as a single recorded by Patti Page (with Jenkins and his orchestra in 1956) and contains the lyric "'Cause when you leave New York, you don't go anywhere."

"Yeah. On my way to a job now," I said, sliding back behind the wheel, waving as I drove off.

I stopped in the next town at a grocery, bought a loaf of bread, cheese, and a bottle of milk—ate in the car from then on. White people are nuts but I'd be even crazier if I got into a fight about it—now.

NOW

6

We were driving along country dirt roads, but carefully. A low-slung Jaguar wasn't made for such roads. I'd about talked myself out, was waiting for her to say something. Her silence made me nervous. When we turned into a paved road Frances asked, "Can I take the wheel? I've never driven a foreign car."

I stopped and we changed places. She drove with cool skill and after a moment said, "What can I do to help you, Touie?"

"The first thing is to understand what you're getting into. I'm wanted, so helping me makes you an accessory to a crime, or whatever the exact legal term is."

"Don't worry about that. All I know is you're a musician and I'm showing you the town."

"It won't be that simple once they start grilling you."

"You talk as if you expect to be caught, Touie."

I spread my palm on my knee. "I did some thinking on the drive here. No point in kidding myself. The New York City police are good, big time. For all I know they've identified me already, have 'wanted' flyers on me in the mails. Honey, I want your help, I need it badly, but at the same time I don't want you in over your head."

"I want to help you. As for the rest—you can't cross a bridge until you reach it." She turned off into a bumpy dirt road.

"Go slow; a rock can rip the transmission."

She drove another few hundred feet and stopped. "What do we do first?"

"Answer a few questions. Has May Russell left town recently?"

"Not that I've heard."

"Would you hear?"

"Yes and no. Actually I haven't seen May for weeks, but in a small town, taking a trip is over-the-fence news. I'd have heard if May left town."

That didn't mean a thing. She could have flown to New York and back in less than an afternoon. "How about her...eh...clients? Have any of them left Bingston recently?"

She grinned. Her mouth was small and the heavy lips seemed to be pouting. "If you believe rumors, every white man in town is a 'client' of May's. I haven't heard of anybody leaving Bingston in months. Tomorrow I'll take you to somebody who can tell you everything you wish to know about May. And a lot about Porky Thomas. What else can we do now?"

I pulled out the TV data, held it near the dashboard light. "When Thomas was in school, he beaned a kid named Jim Harris with a rock, gave him a concussion. Where's Harris now?"

"In South America. He left Bingston years ago, went to college and came out an oil engineer. I know he's still down in South America. Pop saves stamps and takes them off Harris' letters to his folks here."

"Now, in '48 Thomas did a couple of months with a Jack Fulton for petty theft. In '45, he and this same Fulton did a stretch at reform school. Do you know Fulton?"

Frances nodded. "He died in Korea. His name is on the bronze tablet next to the school flagpole. What else?"

I crossed Fulton's name off. The trouble was, there wasn't much "else." "Nothing about it here, but I suppose Thomas was on the lam from the draft too. Was he drafted?"

"I don't know. What's next?"

She sounded like we were playing a quiz game. I put the TV stuff back in my pocket. "That's about it. Are you certain nobody—I mean, anybody who really knew Thomas—hasn't left town in the last month or two?"

"People don't leave Bingston or come to it. Dad would know if anybody has left recently or—Oh, I forgot, the McCall sisters, a couple of old-maid school teachers. They sold their house two months ago and moved to California, but you wouldn't be interested in them. Although when Porky was about ten he was supposed to have pinched Rose McCall's behind."

"He was an all-around cut-up. Look, can you remember anybody Thomas ran around with, or anybody who hated him?"

"Hated? Plenty of people disliked him. I did, he was such a mean cuss, but I don't think most people paid enough attention to him to hate Porky. But this fellow we'll see tomorrow, he can tell you more about that. What else?"

"That's about it, until we see this fellow. Don't look so disappointed—I wish I had more to go on, too."

"Me and my TV mind. I thought we'd be out taking fingerprints and…and stuff like that." She started the Jag, drove very slowly. We made a turn in the rough road and there were a house and a barn silhouetted against the moonlight. She turned the ignition off. "Touie, I don't want to tell you your business, but I think you should get rid of your car. Not many people have seen it, but it's sure to be a sensation in Bingston. This is my Uncle Jim's farm. Suppose I was showing you the countryside and your car broke down?"

"Fine. But how do we get back to Bingston?"

"I'll borrow one of his rattletrap cars. Your Jaguar will be safe here. And don't forget, you're Mr. Jones."

"I won't, Miss Detective." I took a small wrench out of the dashboard compartment, reached under and behind the dash and disconnected the ignition wires, careful not to lose any screws and nuts.

We walked up to the dark house, which proved to be a two-story, ramshackle affair. A couple of dogs came at us, barking. Frances said, "Stand still, they won't hurt you." She began talking to the dogs, baby talk, and they wagged their long tails furiously and gave me a good sniffing over.

A light appeared in an upper window, a flickering lantern light. The window opened and a shotgun barrel appeared, followed by the large head of an elderly brown man who asked, "Who's out there?"

"It's me, Uncle Jim, Frances."

"Oh Lord, something wrong at home? I'll be down in a jiffy."

He shut the window and I heard him shout, "Frances is outside!" and the house filled with sounds and flickering lights.

"Hasn't the electrical age reached here?" I asked, like it was my business.

"That's the big battle in their house. Old Jim is tight, has money's Mammy. He believes what was good enough for him is good enough for the family and the rest of that old—"

The light went on in the room before us, the door opened, and a whole gang of people started out at us. A short stocky old man wearing thick glasses, his bald dark head fringed with gray curls. He was wearing work pants over an old-fashioned suit of heavy underwear. Next to him stood a plump woman with a fat brown face, holding a worn robe about her. Behind them were a husky young fellow in a T-shirt and work dungarees and a bronze-colored, pretty young girl in shiny blue pajamas and blue mules—the rest of them were barefooted. They stared at me in surprise as the woman asked Frances, "Child, what's wrong? Who's dead?" She had a gold tooth in the front of her mouth.

"Nothing's wrong, Aunt Rose," Frances said as we walked in. "This is Mr. Jones, a musician on his way to Chicago. He's stopping at our house. I was showing him the countryside when his car broke down."

"Riding at this hour of the night?" the old lady asked.

"Shoot, ain't no law against taking a ride at any hour," Uncle Jim said, his voice deep, his handshake rough. He introduced me around. The young fellow was his son Harry and the girl in blue Harry's wife.

The old lady said she'd make coffee as Frances asked if they would keep my car in the barn until I got new parts, and could she borrow one of their old struggle-buggys?

Uncle Jim said it was nothing. Harry put on shoes and a worn army jacket with an anti-aircraft shoulder patch, went out with me to push the Jag into the barn. Soon as he saw the car he sighed, "Hot damn!" Then yelled, "Ruth, Ma, Pa, come and look at this here job!"

I smiled in the darkness. It was like a hillbilly cartoon come to life. The entire family trooped out—in shoes—and looked the Jaguar over in the moonlight. I had to make my usual little speech about what a Jag cost new, how many miles per gallon, what speed she could do. Then Harry and I grunted and sweated as we pushed the car up the rough driveway. Frances walked alongside and steered. It was hard work, the barn up on a small hill. Finally Uncle Jim opened the door and we rolled the Jag in. There was a fairly new Dodge in the barn and in the yard behind the barn I saw five or six old cars standing around like wrecks. We were both sweating and puffing and I wiped my face, got my pipe going. Harry was still gazing at the Jag and I said, "Thanks for helping me. Where did you serve in the army?"

"I had it good, never left the States. Stayed mostly in California. Met Ruth there, and brought her back to the farm. She didn't take to it much—at first."

He had it "good." I wondered what he'd think of the farm, of Bingston, if he'd been lucky enough to have been sent to Europe. As he started toward the house I asked, "Did you know this Robert Thomas I was reading about?"

"I used to get along with old Porky pretty good. What's he done now?"

"The papers say he was murdered up in New York City."

"Ole Porky got hisself killed? We haven't been to town to see a paper in days and I didn't hear nothing about it on the radio. Usually not much worth reading in the papers, but this—"

"I thought you knew. You said you *used* to get along with him."

"That was when we were kids. I'd say I ain't seen Porky in around...ten years. After I beat the slop out of him once, he wasn't no trouble."

"The papers said he was a rough character," I said, stopping to relight my pipe, pack it down—stalling before we reached the house.

"He wasn't real bad. A white kid like old Porky, he ain't got nothing, so it make him feel good bossing colored kids. I'd see him in the woods a lot; he was always roaming around, even stealing eggs. To eat, you see. First time I seen him stealing some of our peaches, he called me a name. I was always big for my age, so I slapped him around and he begin to bawl. I never forget him bawling. I told him I don't mind him snitching fruit but he had no call cussing me out. After that, he'd come around now and then and I'd sneak him out some hot food. He always had cigs on him. We'd sit and smoke in the fields and shoot the gas. Of course when he got older I didn't see much of him. You say he's dead? Jeez!"

"You think anybody in Bingston had it in for him?"

"Naw. Who'd remember him or—?"

We were caught in a dim flood of light as the back door opened. Aunt Rose called out, "Harry, what you standing out there in the night cold for? I got food on."

We walked into a huge kitchen with an old pump beside the sink, an old-fashioned round kitchen table, and the largest coal stove I've ever seen. Coffee was brewing, eggs frying, and Ruth was cutting a pan of hot cornbread. I had the feeling this was the first time the family had been up past midnight in years, were making it an event.

Harry said, "Mr. Jones here says he read that old Porky Thomas was killed. It's in the papers."

Frances gave me a bored look and Uncle Jim said, "Guess people are satisfied now. They always said he'd come to a no-good end. Hit by a car?"

"He was murdered, Pa. Up in Chicago."

"New York, the paper said," I said.

Ruth, busy setting the table, said, "If we had electricity here, we could have a TV set and everything. Know what's going on."

"Now Jim said he'd think about it after the summer. Let's just sit and have no arguments," the old lady added, ending the conversation.

We finished off a tremendous amount of food as they questioned me about New Orleans and Chicago, would I have to send to England for parts for the Jag, and the old man fingered my suit and wanted to ask how much it cost but didn't. All this small small talk, the kerosene light flickering overhead, gave everything an air of unreality. Especially the way the old woman was looking me over—with frank disapproval—as if I was Frances's boy friend.

We left about an hour later, Frances driving an old Chevvy with busted upholstery and smelling of chickens. I said I'd be out in a day or two to call for the Jag and everybody shook hands as if we'd finished one hell of a big night.

Frances said, "I'll be at the house for you tomorrow, at lunchtime. I'll take you to see Tim; he can tell you all you want to know about May Russell and Porky. He's May's brother."

"Then he's white."

"Of course."

"I thought we were going to see a friend of yours?"

"Tim is my friend."

I shook my head. "The way you were talking on the way out here, I thought you avoided ofays like the plague."

"Nonsense, there's good whites. Trouble is the bad ones are *so* bad."

"I'll have to explain why I'm asking questions. Suppose I'm a reporter, doing a story on the Thomas killing? No, too soon for that. Think I'll stick to this musician kick—I'm doing the musical scoring and sort of getting the feel of things for the TV show, so I'd be—"

"Stop worrying, you don't have to tell him anything. I told you, Tim's all right."

Her voice sounded sharp. I didn't know what "all right" meant and didn't ask. When we reached the Davis house we saw a light downstairs. Frances said in a weary voice, "Wouldn't you know, Mom is waiting up for me."

"Well, spin around and show her there's no hay on your back."

She drew in an angry breath, glared at me. Or maybe she was startled. I said, "I didn't mean to talk out of turn. Merely a joke, and not very funny."

She laughed, her solemn face coming alive. "I think it's a good gag. Remember about tomorrow, sleep late. I won't be back for you until noon."

"Fine. How far did you say Kentucky is from here?"

"Depends. On the main road, about twenty miles. Why?"

"Okay if I borrow this car?"

"Sure. What's there in Kentucky for you?"

"I'll phone a friend in New York, find out what's playing. In case the call is traced, I don't want anybody to think of Bingston," I said, and it sounded stupid—any map would show the cops how far Kentucky was from Bingston.

We went in and Mrs. Davis was dozing in a stuffed leather chair, didn't hear us. There was a strong resemblance to the old woman on the farm—if she was sporting a gold tooth Mrs. Davis could be taken for a twin sister. I waved good night to Frances and went upstairs as I heard her shake the old lady awake, tell her, "Come on now, Mama, get your sleep. I'm home—all safe and sound. We stopped at Uncle Jim's place for a snack. Mr. Jones' car broke down."

"I always tell you anything flashy isn't any good," the old lady mumbled.

I undressed and stretched out on the bed, feeling wide awake. I lit my pipe and thought what an odd place Bingston was—South and yet not really South. That cop ready to break my head over a simple thing like a cup of coffee, yet when he asked about the Jag he had sounded as friendly as could be. And a chick like Frances, bitter and tough in her own way, yet sticking her neck way out to help me. Why? What was her why? That farmhouse—a little world of its own. And how did a young girl like Harry's wife take to living way out in the country, without electricity, probably no plumbing? Or Harry, how could he return to nothing after seeing California, the big cities, while in the army? If he'd seen Paris, London, Rome—would he still have returned? Sybil would raise hell at the very idea of living there. Me too, probably. Yet, in a way it was a far cleaner world than Harlem, or a big city. There wasn't any Mrs. James being dunned and cheated, or TV programs capitalizing on someone's misfortune to sell drugs. Kay and Bobby, they would seem like people from another planet—out on the farm.

In a sense Uncle Jim was smart—no papers, TV, probably the battery radio didn't work most of the time. Hardly ever saw a white face either. Maybe that was worth kerosene lamps and chicken smells. They reminded me of a Negro couple I once met, middle-aged schoolteachers. They had—maybe still have—an old apartment up in the Bronx. Every summer they both went to Paris and during the winters, the moment they entered their apartment, they spoke only French, ate French food, read Paris newspapers....Soon as they entered their apartment they were no longer Negroes in the Bronx, but back in Paris. Without realizing it, Uncle Jim had done the same thing on his farm, had...

Then it hit me—like when you miss a hard tackle and the earth comes out and pounds everything out of you. I was lying here and thinking about the farm and Bingston as if I was a tourist, a spectator...as if *I wasn't wanted for murder*!

Fear gripped me so hard I had a cramp and had to run to the john in my underwear. What was I really doing here in Bingston, playing detective or playing the fool with my own life? Was the answer to the killing in this sleepy town? In fact, *was* there an answer? Damn, if only I hadn't hit that cop. Suppose I'd let him take me in, told my story—after all, what motive did I have for killing the jerk? With their labs and men, the police would have found the real killer. At least there would be pros working on the case.

But would they have worked on it? Hell, they could say I was sore at Thomas for that coffeepot stuff, came back to kill him. Anything made sense—to whites—when a colored man was involved. A jury wouldn't take my word either....Hell, what was the point in all this IF thinking? No one stands still for a pistol whipping. I had belted a white cop, and I was in this strange little Jim Crow town, with a few bucks, wasting precious time being philosophical about a lousy farm. I was doing nothing for myself. The trouble was I didn't know how I could do myself any good. I was a busher* playing in the big league.

I went back to my room, turned out the light. To my surprise I dozed off, and slept up a storm. The next thing I knew the sun was hitting my face. It was nine o'clock and I felt full of pep. I washed up, considered shaving with the mailman's old-fashioned straight razor hanging beside the medicine chest, then dressed and went downstairs.

Mrs. Davis was in an old print dress, dusting, some sort of crazy lace cap on her gray head. She told me Frances and Mr. Davis had been gone for hours. "We don't sleep our lives away here." I could have told her she didn't know how much she slept away her life but instead I stashed away one of these big country breakfasts—about a million calories in sausages, eggs, and wheat cakes swimming in syrup and butter. The old lady politely grilled me about my family, my busted nose, how long was I staying, had I ever been married. She had coffee with me, telling me the trouble she had with Frances. "That child has such queer ideas, I mean, the way she won't do a thing with her hair, or use powder."

She wanted somebody to talk to and told me about her first child, who had died because she had waited too long to stop

---

* A player in the "bush leagues," the minor leagues that fielded semipro baseball teams and fed talent to the major leagues.

working, how she hoped the son at college would enter medical school after he did his army time.

When I finally pushed myself away from the table at ten, she told me, "I expect money in advance for room and board. Since I owe you a dollar, that will be three dollars for today and tonight."

I gave her three bucks, said I was going to see the country-side and would be back by noon.

"I'll have lunch waiting. Please be careful, Mr. Jones. Remember the customs down here. You know."

I said I knew. The ancient Chevvy shook like a baby's rattle and still stunk, but the motor sounded okay. I stopped "down-town" for a paper, a change of underwear, a razor and tooth-brush, then took off for ole Kentucky. There wasn't anything new in the paper, a rehash of yesterday's account. That didn't mean a thing, the police only give out the news that suits them.

It was a clear day, almost warm, and like a moron I was full of good spirits. I took off my Burberry,* brushed it with my hand, tried to brush the dirty seat with the newspaper, and gave the Chevvy gas. I drove for about a half hour, passing some pretty country. I passed through a few wide-spots-in-the-road, one-store villages, wondered where I was. When I saw a gas station I drove in, asked a young white fellow, "Can you tell me how to get to Kentucky?"

He stared at me; maybe he was looking at my Countess Mara tie.† He said, "You must be new around here, boy."

"Yeah—sir." I almost gagged on the last word. Was it as bad as this for guys in the army to "sir" me?

"You're in Kentucky now. Where you going to?"

"Why…Louisville."

---

* A popular (and expensive) British coat.

† A popular (and expensive) Italian tie maker.

"Better gas up, boy, you got a long ride ahead of you," he said, and started giving me directions. He put in five gallons, told me it was $1.65.

As I took out my wallet I glanced back at the pump meter and his long face flushed as he asked, "What's wrong, boy, don't you take my word?"

I damn near ripped the wallet, I gripped it so hard. Then I gave him a sickly grin as I handed a five-buck bill out the window, said, "I was only looking around to see if you had a pay phone here, chief." I could see a phone booth next to the office; I would have had to be blind not to see it.

"Oh," he said, relieved. As he gave me my change he added, "Keep going down this road a piece; you'll see a dirt road on your right after about a mile. Make a left on that for couple hundred yards. There's a colored store there."

"Thank you, sir," I said, and drove off.

The "colored" store was an enlarged shack with dusty windows that looked like a mild wind would take it apart. Inside there were several rows of canned goods behind a wide counter, a juke box, a wall phone, two homemade tables, and against the rear wall bottles of beer and soda were floating in a washtub full of ice.

A slim fellow with a small sharp face, light brown skin, and wearing worn overalls was leaning on the counter, playing with an empty pop bottle. Behind the counter there was a joker about six-five and at least 350 pounds of fat. But it was fairly well distributed and he carried it so well he looked like an overpadded football player. His face was the size of a pumpkin, dirty tan in color, with a knife scar down one cheek. His oily hair was plastered on his big dome under a stocking cap, and the wool plaid shirt and dungarees he wore must have been made of iron—to withstand the strain of his fat.

When I came in, Slim merely glanced at me out of the corner of one eye, while Fat-stuff asked, "New around here, ain'tcha, boy?"

"Yeah, I'm new and I've heard all the boy-ing I want for the morning. Give me a dollar's change, I want to use your phone."

He ran his eyes over me and didn't move. After a second he said, "I don't like for no dark boys come busting into my store, asking me to do this and that. What you going for, a tough stud?"

For a second I wanted to reach over the counter and take this fat bastard apart, then I relaxed, thinking: Sure, I'd be talking big at the front gate because he's colored. But I kept my mouth going like Charlie McCarthy* sirring that white jerk at the gas station. Be too easy, too ofay, taking it out on this tan slob. I put a dollar on the counter, told him, "Heavy, I don't know you, you don't know me—so don't give me a hard time over nothing. I only came in to make a call. Or don't you have a dollar's change?"

"Sure I got a buck's change. I can change a hundred-buck bill too—any day of the week. Can you?"

"No," I said, patiently.

"That's what I thought. Never saw a stud in fancy clothes that had a full pocket." He decided he'd made whatever point his fat head was bent on proving, dug into his pocket and slapped four quarters on the counter. I walked over to the phone, taking out all my loose change. I had the phone deal figured—I'd reach Sybil at the public phone in the employees' lounge, the way I

---

* Charlie McCarthy was the dummy used by ventriloquist Edgar Bergen (father of Candice Bergen of *Murphy Brown* fame). Bergen achieved great success on the radio; after he made numerous appearances on the stage and other radio shows, the *Charlie McCarthy Show* aired from 1949 to 1955. Though the show failed to transition to television, Bergen and McCarthy were guests on many other television programs. Probably the best-known ventriloquist's dummy in the world in 1957, Charlie's persona was a well-dressed wiseacre.

usually called her to say I'd pick her up. Seemed to me there was no chance of it being traced. With Fatso and Skinny not even making a pretense of not listening, I gave long distance the number, talking in as low a voice as I could. It hardly seemed a second before a girl answered. When I asked for Sybil the girl said she was working. I asked if I could reach her and the girl said to hold on, she'd see.

Another few seconds and the girl said she was still trying to find Sybil. I waited a couple of minutes. The operator told me to signal when through. The tub of lard back of the counter remarked to nobody, "Sure an expensive call you making, Slick. I never seen a man talk so little." He chuckled like a jackass. "All that nothing for so much money."

Finally I heard Sybil's sharp, "Who is this?"

"Hello hon. How's things?"

In a voice low, mad, and hysterical she said, "Touie Moore, you're going to cost me my job! The police came to my house last night!" She gulped as she said the word "police." "And I'm sure a police car followed me to work this morning! Trooping into *my* house…and if the company learns—"

"Slow down, honey. What did the boys say, what did they want?"

"They asked if I knew where you were, when I'd last seen you—That's all."

"That's all? Didn't they say anything more? Did they say what—that is—*why*—they were interested in this fellow?"

"What are you double-talking about? I told you all they said. I was never so embarrassed in my life. I thought it might be you and I was still undressing when I opened the door—you should have seen the way they looked at me."

"What did you tell them?"

"The truth! That I hadn't seen you since the day before, had no idea where you were. Touie, I don't know what you're mixed up in but if you had a normal post-office job—"

"*You don't know?* Honey, haven't you been reading the papers, watching TV, as usual?"

"You louse, are *you* checking up on me? You have your—"

"No, no, I—eh—didn't mean it like that."

"What's wrong with you? You're talking in riddles."

"I'm at a public phone."

"When am I going to see you?"

"I don't know. Soon, I hope. I'll be in touch."

"You listen, Touie Marcus Moore, you pay me back my money. All of it! I must have been crazy letting you take that money. God knows what you're doing with it."

"I'm buying an oil well for Kim Novak,* what else would I be doing with the money? I'll call again. Now take it easy and don't worry."

"I have ninety-four reasons why I worry—!"

"So long for now, honey." I hung up and didn't know what to make of things. Why hadn't the police said anything about the murder, why wasn't it in the papers or on the air? If they visited Sybil, they knew about me, then why the big secret? Damn—if Sybil had been able to think of anything but her money I might have got some news from her. But she didn't know a thing. And how did the cops identify me so damn quick? Kay? Hard to say which side she was on. It had to be the same cat who set me up for the police....Three little letters: w-h-o that could mean my life. K-a-y, three more interesting letters. Although the three letters I really needed were SOS.

The operator rang back to drawl politely that I owed another eighty-five cents. They were slipping down here; hadn't worked

---

* The young, blonde movie star, who appeared in 1957 in *Pal Joey* with Rita Hayworth and Frank Sinatra.

out any way for the operators to know if they were talking to colored, so they could drop the politeness. I told her I'd have to get more change.

I put another buck on the counter and Fatty, who was leaning across the counter, asked, "How you know I got any more change, fancy boy?"

"Your phone. I can walk out and forget the whole thing," I said calmly—I wasn't going to let this fat jerk bug me.

He finally got into motion, made change. As I dropped the coins in and hung up, he said, "Lot of money for just talk. A hot gal, worth—?"

"That was my mother," I said, making for the door.

Lardy was comical as his fat puss changed and he said, "Sorry, boy, I shouldn't have run my month like that. No hard feelings."

I waved as I shut the door. Driving back to Bingston I couldn't make any sense out of what Sybil told me. Of course, if they were keeping it out of the papers, the police wouldn't tell Sybil they wanted me for murder. But from what she said they sounded so damn casual, like they wanted me for skipping a traffic ticket. Maybe they weren't after me for the murder? Nuts, they'd certainly want me for slugging the cop, probably want me worse for that than for a murder. And how could they know "a" Negro was me so damn fast? Who was masterminding all this, if it wasn't Kay? After all, I only had Bobby's word that she had picked me, not Kay....Bobby would say anything to protect Kay. But even if it was Kay, what possible relationship could she have had with a punk like Thomas? And I didn't have time to check on her boss, this B.H....That out-of-town alibi could be bunk. But again, what would a big TV executive be doing with a two-bit guy like Thomas? Of course, there might be an answer to that since in that crowd it was hard to tell who was a "he" or a "she." I never knew how Kay got all the data on

Thomas; suppose her boss did the research, met Thomas and made a pass at him? If Thomas was shaking him down...that could be a motive.

That seemed to fit—a little. That I *thought* Thomas was a hard-working joker leading an uneventful life didn't mean a thing. I'd only seen him a few times. I actually didn't know a thing about him. But if B.H. was a queer and had known Thomas, why didn't Kay get suspicious of him? Or didn't she know about that? Still, why should I expect her to risk her job for me? Even Sybil couldn't think of anything but her lousy money. One thing was for certain—if the cops knew about me, I'd been smarter than I knew leaving New York.

I reached the Davis house before noon, washed and shaved. Frances knocked on my door. She looked very fresh in form-fitting slacks, a simple Italian-style striped blouse cut square across the shoulders—and she had real shoulders, not just bones. She was wearing red ballerina shoes and her hair was in a tight bun, with a kind of pearl necklace around it, the pearls in sharp contrast to her black hair. Her lips were carefully painted a faint red. I watched the lips as she asked, "Did they make you a Kan-tuck colonel?"*

"They gave me a citation for wearing out my gums saying 'sir.' We seeing this Tim Russell?"

"Soon as you're ready. I'll wait for you in the car."

As I put on my tie and coat I heard Mrs. Davis downstairs asking why she was wearing her new outfit and Frances telling the old lady to please keep still. When I walked out, she was

---

* The commission of Kentucky colonel is the highest title of honor bestowed by the governor of Kentucky, and the Honorable Order of Kentucky Colonels is a voluntary philanthropic organization. The title had already become something of a joke by the mid-1950s with the popularity of the Kentucky Fried Chicken fast-food franchises and their founder and spokesperson Colonel Harland David Sanders (who became a Kentucky colonel in 1935).

waiting behind the wheel of the Chevvy. As I got in beside her, Frances started the heap, asking, "Find out anything new?"

"No."

"I spoke to Dad. No one has left town recently."

As we came out of the driveway, a tall slim fellow in work pants, polished boots, and a plaid mackinaw waved at Frances. His hand seemed suspended in midair, and his light brown face with the carefully trimmed mustache showed shocked surprise. She waved back as we turned into the street. He shouted, "Say Frances, I—Hey, wait!"

"No time now," she called back, speeding down the street. "That's Willie."

"The boy friend?"

"My, aren't we the detective. Well, he isn't. I go out with him sometimes—I have to go out with somebody. Matter of fact, because I play hard to get—I suppose—Willie's hinted he might consider marrying me."

"Handsome fellow."

"Willie is the big deal for colored girls in Bingston; quite a catch, and he knows it. He was a paratrooper, the only one in Bingston, so that makes him something, and he has a steady job driving a coal truck, makes good money. He thinks all he has to do is ask and a girl will roll over and wag her tail like a dog begging. I don't think I could stand marrying him. But sometimes...When you're twenty-five Willie can look like all the excitement in the world...from here."

I didn't want to get into her business so I asked, "What am I to tell this Tim? I mean, what am I supposed to be?"

"You don't have to tell him anything. He understands you're in a jam—without asking questions. He was one of the few whites who helped us in the fight to sit in the orchestra of the movie house. He's...I guess you'd call him the town radical. He's a very good guy. At one time I dreamt I was in love with him."

I turned to stare at her. "Then what happened?"

"Nothing. I—we—never did anything about it. He's married now. I soon realized Tim was merely a girlish daydream, I had confused admiration for love."

"This dawn come before or after he was married?"

"Before. Stop teasing me!" She snapped it out the way Kay had told me never to make fun of her.

"Sorry."

We drove through the main street and after a few minutes turned into a muddy field that could have been a baseball diamond. There was a small weather-beaten grandstand we passed as she drove for a group of trees on the other side of the field and stopped next to a parked pickup truck. The guy behind the wheel was about twenty-three, crew-cut yellow hair that reminded me of Thomas', and a lean rugged face with sharp blue eyes. He looked like a middle-weight pug. He was wearing a work shirt and a dirty suéde windbreaker. Frances said, "Hello, Tim. This is Mr. Jones."

He said hello and reached out of the truck window, shook my hand. Maybe he was a pug; he had a dent in his short nose, and a scar over his left eyebrow. "What is it you want to know about my sister?" His voice was dry and plain.

"About the trouble she had with Porky Thomas."

The eyes hardened. "I never called him that. He wasn't a—You're not one of these TV people that were here a month or two ago?"

"No."

"I told them at the time I wouldn't rake up any mud for them. That still goes."

"What was your sister May's reaction to the TV people?"

He ran a stubby hand through his short hair. "Look, Mister, I don't agree with May's ideas on most things, but I try to understand her. May—oh they buttered her up. Called her a promising young singer—she always wanted to be one. They made a recording of her doing a song, said she'd be on TV screens all over the country. She co-operated with them—I'm told."

"You see May much?"

"No. It isn't that we're unfriendly. We're just not friendly any longer. There's a difference."

"Did she leave town a few days ago?"

"No. She's never been out of Bingston, except to go shopping in Cincinnati."

"But since you don't see her, she could have left—?"

"I know she didn't. I thought you wanted to ask about Bob Thomas?"

"I am. Do you know anybody here who might have reason to hate him?"

"Not enough to kill him. After all, he hasn't been around in years. He was forgotten more than hated."

"What was your reaction when you read about his being killed?"

"Me? I don't know, I suppose most of all I felt sorry. We used to live in a shack at the end of town, place called the Hills. Bob lived there with his mother—I never saw or knew his father—and some other poor families. It's a garbage dump now, was then too, but unofficially. The junk heaps gave it the name Hills. There was about seven or eight families lived there, white and colored." He looked across me at Frances. "Fran, you talk to Mrs. Simpson recently?"

"Not for a week or so."

He toyed with his hair again. "Damn health hazard for her. Mrs. Simpson still lives out there. We've been trying to have her move…But you want to know about Bob. He is—was—several years older than May and me. But we three hung out together, hunting rats with slingshots, building shacks…all that kid stuff. Sometimes when his Ma didn't show up for a few days, he'd eat at our place. My mother died when I was a baby and my father was a drunk. I guess he tried to raise May and me the best he could, only it was too much for him, and he kept losing himself in a bottle. What I'm trying to say is—we were a wild bunch of kids, hungry and ragged all the time. When I was nine an uncle came to live with us. He worked as a mechanic, taught me most of what I know about cars. More important, we started eating regularly—until he left a few years later. He liked to move about and—I'm giving you this in detail only because Fran said you wanted a complete picture."

"That's exactly what I need," I said, wondering if lover boy Willie called her Fran.

Tim studied me for a second, as if about to ask why, but he didn't. He said, "Bob used to eat with us a lot. His Ma was staying away more and more. She was a waitress in a dive over in Cincy. It was the end of the depression then and she had a hard time keeping herself fed. May was growing up a real beauty. She was fifteen when our uncle took off and—Mr. Jones, this is damn hard for me to say; I have to make it short. Pop died of exposure that winter and we kids raided farmers' fields, lived like animals. When May began bringing home money I was too young to even suspicion how she got it. Bob was crazy about her and by then they were—well—going steady, I guess you'd call it. Guess you know he did time at reform school after his Ma disappeared and—"

"What happened to his mother?"

"Later we learned she'd been killed in a car wreck over in West Virginia. We stopped a lot of the wild kid stuff. I even started going to school more and when Bob came back from the reform school, he always had a few bucks on him, and told me he was working for a dairy farmer. Of course May was giving him the money. And I knew what she was doing by then, I *had* to know. I tried to stop her. I left school and got a job, but how much can a kid make? Bob, he wanted her to stop, too, but he never held down a job for long. And what could he make? You understand, May wasn't any silly oversexed kid out for thrills. Way she saw it she was—well—she was selling her body, but then what does a factory girl do but sell her arms and legs?"

He paused, perhaps waiting for an answer. I said, "Guess that's one way of looking at it."

"I don't know," Tim said, as if thinking it over. He shook himself slightly. "In '50, when she was nearly seventeen, May found herself pregnant. She wanted Bob to marry her. He was willing but insisted she give up—what she was doing. She couldn't see that. Whenever Bob worked, he only picked up dimes at odd jobs and May had enough of poverty. He refused to marry her. May was getting big and upset about the kid not having a 'name.' Other people were getting worried too. May's 'work' was still pretty much of a secret, even in a small town like Bingston; only a few men were supporting her. Things came to a head when Bob was due to be drafted. She had to do something about her pregnancy—she had him arrested for rape. It was a lousy thing to do but she only did it because she thought it would scare him into marrying her. Needless to say the so-called respectable citizens who were keeping her liked the idea. It was an out for them. You probably know the rest—Bob was released on low bail, to give him a chance to marry May. He beat her so badly she lost the kid, and nearly died. Nobody has seen him here since."

I took out my pipe, lit it. "Did you ever see Thomas again, look for him?"

He shook his head. "If I'd found him that day I would have killed him. I was carrying a hunk of pipe in my pocket to beat his brains out. But I didn't have time to do much looking, I was busy taking care of May. A year later, when I was in the army, I'd try to find him—in whatever town I came to—but I never saw him."

"What would you have done if you had found him?"

He patted his hair nervously. "I don't know. By then, even though I was sending her an allotment, May was working—openly—at her—trade. I think by then I realized it wasn't his fault. He'd been as trapped by circumstances as May. Although he shouldn't have whipped her. I've never forgiven him that."

"Maybe, in his own way, he loved May so much he lost his head," Frances suddenly said.

"Maybe. But I hate violence—for any reason," Tim said. He took out a pack of butts, asked Frances if she wanted one. She said no and he puffed deeply on his, almost savagely.

We were all silent for a moment, then Tim asked, "Have you got a picture of Bob Thomas now, Mr. Jones?"

"Yeah, a pretty good one."

"Odd what you remember about people. Bob always realized his lack of education. When my uncle was living with us, all Bob could do was talk about learning a trade, being a somebody. But then, when he had a little money, I mean May would have put him through a trade school, he never bothered with it."

"In a world of nobodies we all want to be a somebody," I said, almost to myself, thinking Porky Thomas had the desire for a trade till he died.

"What did you say?" Frances asked.

"Just a would-be clever crack from a would-be clever character I know in—eh—Chicago." I turned back to Tim. "Did Thomas have any other brothers or sisters?"

"Nope."

"Was there ever an English teacher employed in the Bingston school named Barbara? Sort of a washed-out-looking woman, probably be between thirty-five and forty now?"

"I never heard of any teacher like that. Matter of fact, Mr. Kraus has been teaching English for as long as I can recall."

"Was Thomas a queer?"

"A what?"

"You know—a pansy?"

"No. I'd never suspect him of that."

"Thomas ran off about six years ago. In all those years hasn't anybody in Bingston seen or heard of him?"

"No. I think they would have told the police, if they had. Not only was there a lot of feeling about the beating he gave May, but most people still think he was the one that got her into trouble."

"But these other admirers of May, suppose they'd come upon Thomas, perhaps tried to take him in and—"

"I don't know a one of them who has left town in years. They all have families here. I think this is about all I can tell you."

"Okay. Would it do me any good to see your sister?"

"She'd scream for the police. Her measure of respectability now is being violently anti-Negro."

"I see. One more question. When the TV people were here, interviewing and taking pictures, didn't that start a lot of talk and renewed interest in Thomas?"

"Damn right there was plenty of talk," he said bitterly. "There still is—everybody waiting to see themselves on the screen. And they were happy to be paid for the interviews—Judas money."

"After you got out of the army, why did you return here?"

He looked surprised. "Why not? It's my town. One of these days May will fall—she's still my sister; I want to be around to pick her up."

I couldn't think of anything else to ask—and he hadn't added much to what I already knew. He started his truck, said, "I hope I've been of some use—for whatever you wanted, Mr. Jones. I'm past due at work." We shook hands and he drove off. At the edge of the clump of trees, where the ground wasn't muddy, he stopped his truck and called Frances. She drove the Chevvy up, got out and they whispered for a moment, then Tim Russell drove on.

As Frances got back in the Chevvy, she said before I could ask, "He wanted to know if you were a cop. I said you weren't."

She waited until his truck was out of sight down the road before starting the Chevvy—I knew they'd met like this before. I asked, "Has Tim got any other brothers, any other relatives in Bingston, or anyplace else?"

"No. Except for his uncle—I vaguely remember him, a stooped old man. I don't think Tim has seen him since he was a kid."

"Can you see Tim again, find out if he knows where the uncle is now, his name?"

"I'll ask him. Do you think the uncle might have done it?"

"Honey, I don't think anything. I'm like the bear—nowhere.* Tell me, do you see Tim around, I mean every day?"

"Yes. I told you, he owns a small garage."

"Are you sure he was in Bingston three days ago?"

---

* According to Eric Partridge's *Dictionary of Catch Phrases* (New York: Stein and Day, 1976), "Like Jack the Bear: just ain't nowhere" means "A US negroes' catchphrase of ca. 1930–1950, indicating extreme disappointment or frustration or wounded vanity." Partridge's source is Clarence Major's *Black Slang: A Dictionary of Afro-American Talk* (London: Routledge & Kegan Paul, 1971). "Jack the Bear" was a popular (wordless) song recorded by Duke Ellington and his Famous Orchestra in 1940—did the song spawn the catchphrase? More likely, Ellington chose the catchphrase as the title, playing off the hipster's use of the term "nowhere" as meaning naïve or clueless.

Like a lot of rhyming slang, the "Jack the Bear" reference probably doesn't mean anything inherently—it just rhymes. For example, in Cockney rhyming slang, "apples and pears" (shorthanded "apples") means stairs, just because pears rhymes with stairs!

She looked away from the road to stare at me with solemn eyes for a second. "He's not the killer, Touie. And I know he was here. He comes into the bakeshop every afternoon on his way home to buy bread and cake, so—I'm due at the shop right this minute. What are you going to do now?"

"I don't know." I didn't have idea one about where to turn. I was standing still while time was rushing by me, running out.

"If you want, I can call in sick, help you."

"Thanks, but I'd better drop you off, then I'll go back to the house, try to think. Does Tim see May now?"

"Very rarely. When he came out of the army he wanted her to give up her—business, move away and start life over again with him. He'd saved up a thousand dollars and he figured he could buy a little garage anyplace. May laughed at him. She offered to set him up in a gas station that cost ten thousand. That was the lick* with them."

She stopped in front of a small frame building with an apartment over a bakeshop with a large window, everything painted white, looking very clean. When Frances got out, I shoved over behind the wheel, feeling her warmth still on the seat. She asked, "Will I see you at supper?"

"Yeah. Look, when you speak to Tim, also ask about Thomas' father. I gather he was a bastard, but find out if Tim has any idea who the father was, where he lived, and if he thinks Thomas ever knew him."

"I'll ask, but I'm sure Porky never knew his father. Anything else?"

"Yes—thanks for giving me your lunch hour."

She smiled as she waved, and I watched her walk into the store. I drove to the Davis house, turned into the driveway and

---

* In the sense of a small amount, meaning that this was the "last straw."

parked. The old lady came to the window, pulled back the lace curtains and nodded at me. I tipped my hat at her, then took out the TV data on Thomas, went over it again. Bingston was adding up to a large zero. As a real detective I was another bust. I kept staring at the papers the way I'd seen detectives do in the movies. I didn't have a smell of a hint, much less a clue. God, how I wished this were all a movie!

Still, unless it was one of these sudden dumb killings, there's always a hell of a good reason for murder, and that reason had to be someplace on this list. Thomas was on the loose for a half a dozen years but was killed when the TV people got interested in his case, so...So what? For all I knew Thomas could have had something going for him in New York. Could have had a fight with his girl friend and she conked him? Only how could she have known about Kay, about me? But Ollie said a girl had phoned—could it have been her? Only she didn't look like a killer—as if I knew what a murderer looked like, as if anybody does. Suppose Thomas took her up to his room, made a pass, and she grabbed the pliers? But that didn't explain how she could know about me and Kay. I kept coming back to Kay. For all I knew the whole TV thing could be a lie...she'd paid me in cash, I didn't even know for sure that she actually worked for Central, or any TV studio. No, no, there was a TV program, they'd interviewed people here.

I kept trying to think things out and only came up with a headache and one sad fact that was for true—as a detective I was a pitiful amateur. And as the old saying goes, I sure had a damn fool for a client.* I'd been crazy to think I...

Mrs. Davis opened the front door. "Want your lunch, Mr. Jones?"

I nodded and climbed out of the car, brushed my coat with

---

* The proverb states, "A lawyer who represents himself has a fool for a client."

my hands. The old lady said, "I suppose Frances took you to a garage to see about fixing your car?"

"Yeah. They're sending to Cincinnati for parts," I said, following old nosey to the kitchen.

"I have some nice hash I've just made, or you can have a slice of ham, fresh rice pudding, coffee or tea. Do you want a towel? You can wash up at the kitchen sink."

The old lady spooked me; all this small talk about lunch as if this was just another afternoon, as if I wasn't wanted for murder. I had nothing on my mind but to decide between hash and ham!

But what could I do, where else could I look? Somehow I had expected this Tim would give me a lead. I always read that when a cop was stuck he started digging into the case again. But everything was so open in this, where could I dig? Where...?

"If you like, you can have hash *and* some ham, Mr. Jones."

"I'll...eh...just a glass of milk, Mrs. Davis."

"Oh come on, a man as big as you needs more than milk to carry him. Still two dollars a day for meals, so you might as—"

"I'm full of breakfast. A glass of milk, if you have it."

"As you wish."

The only thing left was to see some of the people who had been interviewed. Start with people who knew Thomas as a child. What was the name of the old gal Tim said still lived on the garbage dump? I reached for the data sheets in my pocket, remembered Mrs. Davis was around. Sipping the cool milk I said, "Noticed an old shack out by the garbage dump. Anybody living there?"

"Crazy Ma Simpson. Only thing that will ever force her to move from that filth will be death."

"White woman?"

"I'm ashamed to say she's one of our people. I declare, she

could have easily moved long ago, they even found another place for her, but like I said, she's so old, she isn't all there."

I put the empty glass on the table. "Think I'll take a drive."

Mrs. Davis rubbed her hands together, as if she'd heard good news, gave me a knowing smile. "I once saw a show on the television about you musicians, but I never really believed you were all so restless. The music beat must get into your blood, I suppose, like an electric current."

I started for the door. "Guess you're right," I said, wishing she'd stop talking about electricity in my blood—it could so easily come too true.

I drove toward the main street, then turned right, toward the side of town I hadn't seen yet. There were a few cars on the road and as I reached the end of town I could see the "Hills" of garbage ahead of me. A truck passed me, cut in sharply and came to an abrupt halt. I almost put the brake pedal through the floor as the Chevvy spun around, headed for the road shoulder. I wrestled with the wheel, praying the car didn't turn over, and it was a happy prayer. For I knew it all had been deliberate, and if I couldn't find the killer...at least he was finding me.

7

As the Chevvy hit the soft shoulder, tires and brakes screaming,
I got the wheel under control, swung sharply toward the road.
The old car seemed to shiver and dip, then skidded another few
feet to a stop. The truck driver was a bold cat. He'd stopped a few
feet down the road and was watching me in his fender mirror. I
jumped out of the car and ran toward the truck—and slowed to
a walk. Lover boy Willie jumped down from the truck, hitched
up his pants, and came toward me, the high shine on his boots
sparkling in the sun.

I cursed him for being the village idiot under my breath,
knew before he opened his silly mouth all this had nothing to
do with Thomas—he was jealous of my being with Frances. I
asked, "What do you think you're trying to do, junior?"

His tan face flushed at the "junior," but his eyes had the sullen
cast of a pug. Not that I was worried. In a ring maybe Willie
might take me but in a free-for-all I was too much for him. He
said, "Watch your fat tongue, heavy. You ought to know how to
drive. I hear you're a hot rod with a foreign racing heap."

"One of us doesn't know how to drive. If this is meant to be a
big joke, I'm not for laughs."

His smile showed even, very white teeth. He was a joker who gave the mirror a lot of time. "Maybe I was trying to see if you can take it. I don't go for no cat moving in on my time. Especially a stooge in fancy clothes. Frances may—"

The word stooge hit me where I lived. I was a prize dummy— there was somebody else in on the Thomas publicity deal I hadn't even thought of! Kay had said something about having a "stooge planted" to blow the whistle on Thomas after his case appeared on TV. That meant the stooge had to be in on things, that he—or she—either knew all about me, or was in a position to find out easily. Suppose he had crossed the TV people, tried shaking Thomas down, and it had ended in a fight? But that didn't add. Thomas didn't have dime one. Hell with *why*; main thing was to find out *who* the stooge was and then see…

I was watching Willie without seeing him, my mind racing, and now he was hitting me on the shoulders and neck with the side of his right hand, yelling, "Knew you'd chicken out!"

The "blows" didn't hurt and I thought he was having a fit, at first, and then I got it: this clown was giving me the side of his hand as a Judo chop—which can break a bone, even kill you, if done right. It must have been something he'd learned as a para-trooper, only never learned right. I kicked his right boot above the ankle hard as I could. As he howled and bent over to grab his right leg, I kicked the left ankle out from under and he sat down hard, moaning, trying not to scream.

"There you are, Willie, no hands. Not that it's any of your busi-ness, but Frances is merely showing me the town. Keep polishing your boots and out of my hair, or I'll really work you over, maybe even dirty your boots—with you." I walked back to the Chevvy and drove off, keeping an eye on him via the rear window for a moment. I hoped I'd put the proper fear of God into Willie. A jerk behind a wheel is more dangerous than if he had a gun.

I left him sitting at the side of the road, still holding his ankles. I was feeling high about the stooge idea, then it fell down hard. One thing was for positive, I couldn't learn who the stooge was in Bingston. It meant returning to New York, seeing Kay, and she made me uneasy. There were too many unexplained coincidences pointing toward her. I might try phoning her, but that would be a hell of a risk. I let the stooge idea remain in the back of my mind, for more thinking. In a sense it was reassuring, proved I had to keep digging into the case, that I would come up with something. Or was I merely being a fool and digging my own grave?

Bingston burned its garbage, and the Hills was a smouldering field of great heaps of tin-can skeletons, broken bottles, and other unburnable objects. Every couple of months a bulldozer probably stacked the current garbage into a new pile. There was an odd, musky odor you smelled as soon as you neared the dumps, the mysterious stink of decay and death.

About a hundred yards off at right angles from one of the old garbage heaps—some sort of green weeds were growing on it—stood this small wooden shack, bleached by the sun and weather, unpainted for the last hundred years, if it ever had known paint. The windows were covered with newspaper and cardboard; a faint trickle of smoke was coming from the cock-eyed brick chimney sagging against the back of the house. A broken step took me to a small porch with two busted rocking chairs on it. From the porch the garbage heaps seemed to be inching toward the shack like a glacier of waste.

Mrs. Simpson was a surprise, very cheerful and neat. She was a butterball of an old woman, her gray hair in tiny thick braids all over her head, not a wrinkle in her plump dark face, but a ragged faint white mustache over the toothless mouth and a foggy cataract over one eye. Her sweater and plain dress were clean and newly ironed and she padded around in new sneakers. The room I opened the door on—most likely the only room in the shack—was a museum of broken furniture, a coal stove, a working fireplace, bundles of junk, an oil lamp, and a spotless wide bed with a very white spread. Of course the garbage stink was everywhere.

Mrs. Simpson, who could have been eighty, ninety, or a hundred, spoke in a thin drawl as she said, "Come in. Long time since I've had such a fine strapping buck call on me. Come in, boy."

She nodded toward a chair held together by wire and rope and which fooled me by not collapsing as I cautiously sat on it. "My name is Jones, Mrs. Simpson. I'm a writer and—well, I'm trying to do a true-fact crime story on this Thomas killing. You know, while it's news. I thought you might be able to tell me something about Porky Thomas."

"I know about you, the musician man staying at the Davis house," she squeaked, sitting in a rocker and fixing her good eye on me. "Seems like they paying too much attention to Porky, now. Had people down here with lights and cameras asking about him. Took movie pictures of me and my house. Too bad they didn't pay him all that mind when he was younger."

"Tell me, what sort of a man was he?"

"Man? I never knew Porky as a man. I knew him as a child, a white child."

"How did he get along with colored people?" I asked, trying to get her talking. "I know you all lived together here at one time."

"Used to be houses not a stone's throw from here. We all used the same pump and outhouse. Now they want me to move. Why? I ask 'em. I'm too old to move. My children are dead or gone, I'm alone, why should I uproot myself? Nobody said move when I was younger. Do you know I was born a slave?"

The old gal must have witnessed half the history of our country in her lifetime, but I had no time for history now. "What about Thomas, did he—?"

"Don't be impatient, boy. Ain't often I get the chance to talk to people. Why, many is the time, in the old days, when young Thomas slept right in this room, on a mat before the fire. Many is the meal I gave him. He used to get me wood from the dump, build a fire for my washing. He only became mean when he got older, when things turned so bad for him."

"How was he mean?"

"White-mean. About the last I seen of him, maybe a few months before he got hisself in all that trouble with May, I awoke in the night to find the one window I had was busted. There he stood, outside my house, another rock in his hand. He was drunk back. He used to try to be a hard drinker, but he never was. Most times he was acting drunk because I know a few drinks made him sick. I stood in the doorway and asked why he'd busted my window and he says, 'What are you going to do about it, you ole nigger?' So I said nothing, just looked at him hard. He come closer, this wild whiskey look in his eyes. I wasn't scared of him, I never was. Walked right up to me, he did. Then he drops the rock and begins to bawl. Cried like a child. He says, 'Ma Simpson, can I please have a glass of water?' Always called me Ma. I got him water and he took out a handful of money, give me five dollars to fix the window, says how sorry he is. That's the last I ever did see of him. Crying like a child."

"What about the troubles he got into? I mean, before the business with May?"

The old woman pulled out a tin snuffbox, put some under her lip. "They was real nice children, the Russell kids. Tim still drops by. After me to move, but he means well. Porky wasn't in any real trouble, never. Before he beat on May. He did a lot of things young boys do, but seemed he was always caught. If he stole it was only because he was needing things so bad. Ask me, he was meaner when he come out of that reform school than before he went in. I do recall how—after he come out of this reform place—he slapped Mamie Guy and her husband beat Porky up something terrible. Of course none of that got to the police. He'd stole some shirts from Mamie and was angry because she accused him to his face."

"Who's Mamie Guy?"

"Lives out on Beech Road. Shucks, when I was a girl coming along, wasn't even a house or road there, just woods and woods. Nice for picnics and—"

"Mamie Guy still live there?"

She sighed. "You just won't let a person finish a sentence. I had to give up my washing; pains in my legs and shoulders was getting fierce. I gave her my customers. Porky, he was helping me, delivering and calling for the laundry on an old beat-up bicycle he'd put together. So he begin helping Mamie; her boys was too young to help her then. He took these expensive silk shirts, tried to say Mamie had done it. But it was all straightened out."

"Where does Mamie's husband work now?"

"Last I hear he was doing porter work in one of them big stores downtown."

"Who else did Porky ever have a serious fight with? Is there anybody else who hated him?"

"Sam Guy never hated him. Nobody did, just didn't pay no attention to Porky."

"Did he ever knife or pistol-whip any one, seriously hurt somebody? Even another kid?"

"No siree. Porky wasn't real bad. I seen plenty young ones wild like him who settle down to a good life. Ask me, I think

May made a mistake in not marrying him. I mean, before she had to."

I couldn't think of any more questions. I stood up. She rocked back and forth as she said, "A welcome sight to see a black man dressed good like you. All the washing and ironing I done, I know expensive duds."

I thought, "Yeah, I'll be the best-dressed man in the hot seat," as I said, "Well, good day, Mrs. Simpson. Thank you for your time."

She got to her feet. "A colored writer, my how times have changed. Now, like I told those other people, don't make Porky out a bad one. It wasn't he was good nor bad, just so hungry poor. Now that he's dead I know the Lord will give him a better time up there."

Out on the porch I asked, "Does Tim Russell come to see you every day?"

"Oh my no. Maybe once or twice a month. Matter of fact I ain't seen him for couple weeks now. He drives me to town, helps me shop."

"Does he leave Bingston often?"

"Tim leave here? I should say not, except for the time he was a soldier."

I said good-by again and headed for town. My brain was going in circles. I was still wondering who the "stooge" might be, what motive he could have for killing Thomas. And for some reason I was amazed at Mrs. Simpson being so hale and full of cheer despite all the hard work she must have known. I couldn't remember if the local paper had two editions, so I parked on the main drag and went into the tobacco shop. It was the same paper I'd read in the morning. As I stepped back into the Chevvy, the cop I'd run into when I first hit this burg, and maybe Bingston's *only* cop, called from across the street, "Hey there, boy, I want to see you."

I knew a "wanted" flyer had finally reached him and my guts started churning—until I saw the lazy way he was ambling across the street. He said, pleasantly, "Hear that pretty car of yours broke down. Puzzles me: America makes the best darn cars in the world, like this old Chevvy still gets you places.... Like I told the wife, why should a body buy a foreign car and pay so much more money?"

"I got a buy on mine, secondhand." Bingston was a damn goldfish bowl. I had to clear out of here fast. It was, or could be, as dangerous for me as New York. At least in New York I could be checking on this stooge angle. In Bingston I was a sitting duck.

"Me, I don't even hold much with the new cars coming off the Detroit assembly lines today. Too much fancy stuff on 'em. Waste of money."

"I suppose so," I said, wanting to say something about Thomas, that I'd read about it in the papers. But I didn't have the nerve. The N.Y.C. police must have some kind of contact with Bingston, and the last thing I wanted was to get this hick cop interested in me.

He asked, "Think you can get your car fixed soon?"

"Expect to...sir. I'm having a part sent here air mail." I waved and he nodded, as if dismissing me, and I drove off.

I parked outside the bakery. Through the window I watched Frances waiting on a customer, the pleasant contrast of her white work jacket and her warm brown skin. When the customer left I honked the horn. Frances waved at me, then said something to the elderly white woman camped on a high stool behind the cash register. They argued for a moment, then Frances came rushing out, asked, "Did you learn anything new, Touie? I can only stay a second."

"Nothing, except that I have to leave Bingston."

"Why?"

"Far as the killing goes, I'm running in circles here, going noplace. Bingston isn't even a good hideaway; everybody in town knows I'm here, even about my car 'breaking down.'"

"Where will you go?"

"Back to New York, I guess. I've thought of something that needs looking into there."

"But they're looking for you in New York. Touie, why leave at all? People know about you here because you're a stranger. If you remained here and found a job, as Jones, you'd soon be forgotten—I mean, wouldn't stand out. As you said, the New York police are looking for 'a' Negro. Once you became a part of the community here, you'd be safe. They certainly aren't looking for 'a' Negro in Bingston."

The woman in the bakeshop knocked on the window.

"No dice. I phoned somebody in New York this morning; the police already know I'm *the* Negro. In time they're sure to contact Bingston, if they haven't already. Main reason I came here was to find the killer. All I've found was that Thomas was a mixed-up kid."

"If the police know about you, then to go back to New York seems—" She turned sharply and nodded at more knocking on the window. "When are you leaving?"

"Thought I'd go out to the farm and pick up my car, leave now."

"Touie, at least wait until I come home at five thirty. Let's talk about this. All right?"

"Okay."

"Tim should be in soon, and I'll ask about his uncle, and Thomas' father. I have to run now. Not a customer in the store and she's wearing her knuckles out on the window. See you at the house in about an hour." She went back into the shop.

I headed for the Davis house but I was too nervous to sit around. I turned off at the nearest side street, drove aimlessly. I'd better get rid of the Jaguar. Take it from the farm, so they wouldn't get into any jam, if I was caught, ditch it in some river or lake. Although it would break my heart to do that. In New York I could get a room in the colored section of Brooklyn, or the Bronx—although I didn't have much money, in fact no money if I took a train back to New York. Maybe I could get a job, anything, that would keep me eating for a week or two, while I checked on the stooge, Kay's boss, and Thomas' girl in the cafeteria. Damn, if I could only sell the Jag, be enough dough to keep...

I passed a dirt road and a dirty white sign on a metal post that read: BEECH ROAD. Backing up, I turned into the road. It seemed to be all woods until I passed a few new and neat-looking ranch houses, and after another couple hundred yards a weather-beaten shack with a new tarpaper roof, the remains of a fence. A colored kid about twelve was sitting in the yard with his back to me. I stopped the Chevvy and walked back to the yard. Suddenly there was a coughing sound, exactly like a mortar shell going off. I looked around wildly, was so startled I nearly hit the ground.

The kid was watching a bright red rocket about a foot long hissing up through the air. It went a few hundred feet high, did a cockeyed somersault, then came spiraling down to the ground at the boy's feet.

"What's that?"

He jumped as he turned to stare at me, a solemn-faced youngster in a worn sweater and torn dungarees and patched shoes. "Whatcha think it is? It's a rocket." He touched a small plastic stand. "This is my rocket launcher. Pip, isn't it?"

It was a crazy scene: the shack that probably hadn't changed since it was built before the Civil War, and the sleek little rocket.

He opened a paper bag, showed me some white powder. "I put a charge of this atomic fuel in the launcher, add water, and when the reaction reaches its prime I release the rocket. Came in the mail today. Cost me four bucks but—Hey, Mister, you live around here?"

"No. Does Mrs. Mamie Guy live on this road?"

"You bet. Keep going and you'll see a house on the other side of the road. Be lot of clothes hanging on the lines." He lowered his voice. "You know my folks?"

"No."

"Well, if you should meet them, don't say anything about this rocket. I worked extra and saved to buy it, but my Pop would whale me if he knew. Someday I'm going to build a big one, take me to the moon."

"What's so special on the moon?"

He looked at me with disgust, then sat down with his back to me, said, "Blast off, Mister."

I headed toward the car. In a minute there was the slight cough again and the rocket shot high into the air, flying in an arc. It came down several hundred feet away in the leaves of a tall young tree. The kid ran over and started throwing stones at it.

"Why don't you climb up after it?" I called out.

"It's Pop's new pear tree. May break and then I'd really get it. Mama's due home in half hour. I got to work fast."

I walked over to him. The tree was about a dozen feet high, the trunk a few inches thick. I grabbed the trunk and shook it. The rocket fell to a lower branch. I shook it again but it didn't budge. "How much do you weigh?"

"Sixty-three pounds."

"Think you can hold yourself straight if I lift you?"

"You bet."

"Now hold yourself rigid, or you'll fall and break both our necks." I squatted, grabbed him around the waist and took a deep breath—as if getting ready to jerk and press a barbell. I got the kid up to my chest, then held him up at arm's length. He reached up and pushed the rocket out of the branches. I dropped him to my chest, then to the ground.

"Gee, you're strong, Mister."

"Launch that in a field the next time," I said, brushing my coat, wiping the sweat from my face.

He followed me back to the car and as I drove off he asked, "What's your name?"

"Captain Video,"* I called back and had to grin. Big deal: the murderer was captured knocking a rocket ship out of a pear tree.

The Guy house wasn't far down the road, and a copy of the other shack except it was bigger and in better condition. Clotheslines zigzagged all over the yard, with a few sheets swaying in the wind like sails.

A thin dark woman came to the door. Her hair was uncombed and her face sweaty. She could have been thirty, or forty-five, the work-worn look all over her. "My name is Jones. Mrs. Simpson told me you knew Porky Thomas," I said, going into my pitch about being a true-crime writer.

"I have nothing to say. I told them television people once, I ain't got time to make mud fly. I don't believe in snooping into other people's lives." She shut the door.

At least she didn't know I was staying at the Davises' or that I had a Jaguar. "Mrs. Guy, I'm not with any TV studio. I only want to ask a few questions."

"Ask somebody who has time for loafing. I have work to do."

"Can I talk to your husband?"

---

* A popular live television show for children that ran from 1949 to 1955, in which "Captain Video" and his "Video Rangers" had adventures in the distant future.

"That's up to him. He ain't home now."

I stood there for a moment, lit my pipe. Walking back to the car I saw the rocket kid watching me. He said, "Aunt Mamie is cross on the days when she does her heavy washing. You want to talk to her real bad, Mister?"

"Yeah."

He called out, "Aunt Mamie." She came to the door a moment later. "What you want, Kenneth? You know I'm rushed today."

"This is a nice man, Aunt Mamie. I was stuck up in a tree and he stopped his car to help me. Yes he did."

She wiped her wet hands on her gray dress. "I'm wasting more time *not* talking to you. All right, come in, if you want."

The kid winked at me. "Guess I'd best go home and hide my rocket good. So long, Mr. Video."

The kitchen of the shack had several irons heating on the big coal stove, and smelled of damp starch. She pointed to a chair between two wicker baskets of clothes, said, "You can sit there. Only reason I'm talking to you is because you're colored. That's the truth. I didn't even open the door to those TV people. Ought to mind their business, that's what. I hear Porky was killed." Her voice was as thin as her body.

"That's what I want to ask about, Mrs. Guy."

"You wasting my time. He used to deliver laundry for me, but that was a long time ago, when my Edward was born, and he's going on ten now. I ain't seen hide nor hair of Porky since then, and just as well."

"Mrs. Simpson told me he stole some shirts from you, slapped your face."

"That old talking machine. Yes, he did take two silk shirts from a bundle he was delivering. And he did slap me when I accused him of it. But my husband took him down a peg, and that was all. Porky even continued working for me for a time, then he quit me."

"Did he have any enemies in Bingston—before the business with May Russell?"

She shrugged her bony shoulders. "None special. What you driving at, Mr. Jones?"

"I thought somebody from around here might have gone to New York and killed him."

"Folks here got more to do with their time than that. Lot of people didn't like him. I never trusted him, myself. But nobody would kill him. That's all I know. I got ironing to do. All these damn sheets got to be ironed so my husband can take them over to Kentucky after supper."

I stood up. "Thanks for your time. People come all the way from Kentucky to give you laundry?"

"Shucks, all the way is less than twelve miles. I got all the work I can handle. Nobody does clothes like Mamie Guy. Especially delicate things. I never tore anything in my life. Them silk shirts Porky took a liking to, they was from a Kentucky family. Tell you the truth, the shirts was too small for him. He took 'em out of spite and meanness, get even with his cousins. It was McDonald shirts."

"I didn't know he had any relatives," I mumbled, the name McDonald hitting me like a Joe Louis left.

"Not many people know the McDonalds is sort of distant cousins to Porky, on his mother's side, of course. I never heard about it myself, till he took them shirts. They never had no use for either him or his mama, never would even recognize 'em. Shame too, because they always been well off, might have helped the boy when he was running around hungry and raggedy-assed. McDonalds been having a big store over in Scotville* far back as I can recall."

---

* A fictitious town.

"Is one of the McDonalds named Steve?"

"There's Stephen and Ralph, and the girl, Betty. They all left except Ralph. He took over the store when his daddy had a stroke."

"What's Stephen doing?"

"Now mister, how would I know? I only do their washing, don't have tea with 'em. They all went off to college. Betty is married and living someplace out West. Like I said, Ralph, he's married and running the store. Stephen, he ain't been around since after the war. Look, I got to catch up on my work. I got supper to make, too."

"I won't keep you, Mrs. Guy. Is there a phone around anyplace I can use?"

"Take a right at the next fork. Come to Mr. Jake's gas station. He lets colored use his phone."

I thanked her again, sincerely thanked her, then sped toward the gas station like that well-known bat. As Ollie would say when a horse came in for him, I was getting "well."

"Mr. Jake" turned out to be an old white man with liver spots on his face, and a game leg. When I asked if I could use his phone, he nodded toward a wall phone inside his office, said, "That's what it's there for, if you got a dime." I told him to fill the tank, see if I needed any oil—to keep him busy. Scotville was only a fifteen-cent call, and when I got the McDonald store I asked for Stephen and a man said, "I'm Ralph McDonald, his brother. Who is this?"

"I was with Steve in the army—during basic training. I happened to be driving through and wanted to say hello to him."

"Steve hasn't been home in several years. He's a writer in New York City, doing very well."

"Come to think of it, he always talked about wanting to write.

Happens I'm on my way to New York—how can I get in touch with Steve there?"

He told me to call him care of Central TV and wouldn't I like to drop over to his house now for a drink and supper? I said I'd take a rain check but was in a big rush at the moment, and nearly laughed out loud thinking what would happen *if* I should stick my dark face in the McDonald doorway!

I said good-by and hung up. He hadn't even asked my name. I was singing as I raced back to the Davis house. If I left at once, I could be in New York by tomorrow afternoon, but in the Jag I'd be as conspicuous as if I were wearing a red suit. A train would be faster and safer. When I solved things I could come back for the car, and if I didn't, I sure couldn't take the Jag with me.

Mr. Davis was sitting in the living room, feet in slippers, smoking a cigar and reading a magazine. I told him, "I've phoned Chicago and they have to send to England for the part to my car. So I'm leaving now. I have a supper-club job set for Chicago, and I'll return in a few weeks for the car, when I get the parts. What do I owe you?"

"I'll have to ask Mama. Maybe we owe you; she tells me you've hardly eaten here. All rested up now, Mr. Jones?"

"Rested? Sure, sure. Is there a bus leaving here soon?"

"The Cincinnati bus leaves downtown at six fifteen. Should be plenty of trains from there to Chicago."

I went upstairs and took a shower. Then I straightened up with the old lady, who insisted I have a fast supper. I bulled with Mr. Davis about working as a mailman—he seemed to think it was the most useful job ever made. Around five thirty I was getting jumpy and then Frances came home and said she'd drive me to the bus station. One of these mild and pointless family arguments started, the old lady saying Frances should eat supper first and Frances saying she wasn't hungry and Mrs. Davis asking if she was sick. Finally the mailman said to let Frances go but to stop driving around in that rattletrap that belonged on the farm, to take *their* car, which turned out to be a '52 Dodge with only eleven thousand miles on it. I said good-by and Mrs. Davis suddenly asked where my bags were and I said I'd sent them ahead.

Frances seemed to be in a bad mood. She told me Tim had no idea who Thomas' father was, nor where his own uncle was. We parked across the street from the drugstore, which was also the "bus station," and had twenty minutes to kill. For a while we didn't talk but I was bubbling over with the McDonald thing and told her about it.

She said, "Suppose I drive you to Cincinnati, Touie?"

"How far is it?"

"Seventy-four miles."

"Means you'll have to drive 150 miles."

"I don't mind."

"No honey, it's too much." She was staring straight ahead and I stared at the dark profile of her face, which seemed strong and pretty—and angry. "Look, I want you to know, no matter what happens, I won't forget what you did. You're a wonderful girl."

"Thanks." Her mouth was a pretty, thick red line, and the dashboard light did things to the high cheekbones, lighting the skin to a delicious brown. "Don't worry about your car, it will be safe. When do you think you'll come back for it?"

"Soon as I can." When I came back I'd bring her a pair of big silver loop earrings. She had the face to carry them.

"Are you sure this McDonald did it?"

"I'm not sure of anything. There's also another angle I have to look into, but this is a hell of a lead, the best offer I've had. It's too much of a coincidence not to mean something."

"But why should he kill his own cousin?"

"I don't know the motive, but I'll soon find out."

"How?"

"Don't know that either."

"You might be walking into the arms of the police."

"If I do, you have yourself a Jaguar."

"I don't see the joke, Touie," she said sharply.

"Fran, I'm a long ways from home yet on this. It can still add up to nothing, but it's all I have to work on. And if I'm joking—as the saying goes, I'm only laughing to keep from crying. I'll be careful...." A bus was coming down the street. "This mine?"

"Yes."

"Do I have to sit in the back?"

"No."

We walked over to the bus and I squeezed her hand and thanked her again, then I got on, bought a ticket, sat down toward the rear. I waved to Frances, blew her a corny kiss. She seemed about to say something, then she turned away and stared at the drugstore window.

As the bus started I looked back and she was waving. In the split-second last look I had, I thought she was crying.

8

I reached New York early in the morning, feeling good. I'd slept most of the way, sometimes dreaming of Mrs. James and Sybil and Frances. I also had a plan of operation.

I breakfasted at a luncheonette in the station, bought up all the morning papers, retired to a pay booth in the men's room to read them. There wasn't a thing about the killing. A guy has to be rich, or a big shot, to last more than a brace of days in the headlines. Or a woman—for some reason people are interested in reading about dead women.

Of course that didn't mean the cops weren't working like beavers looking for me. At nine I left my tile office, played with the idea of phoning Sybil, but didn't want to hear her wailing about money again. I had a lot of hours to kill and being out on the street made me uneasy. I took a subway up to the Paramount and got in for the early-show price. They lost money on me; I was still there at four in the afternoon. I knew the lines in the movie better than the actors, and was stuffed with popcorn and soda. At four I took a cab to Ted Bailey's office, planted myself across the street. Fortunately Ted came out alone, on his way home. I hailed another cab and picked him up before he reached the subway. Ted was dressed in his usual drab style: a gray suit that didn't fit him, an old overcoat, and a new striped tie he wore like a medal. I told the cabbie to keep driving around the block.

Ted said, "What's wrong with that jazzy car you had, Toussaint? You crash it?"

"Having it checked. What's new?"

"Same old stuff. Mrs. James came through with the money. You must be doing well, cruising around in a cab."

"It isn't the salary but the tips that keep me going," I said, a kind of inside joke Ted didn't get. "I'm on a big divorce case with an expense account a yard wide."

"Money involved, huh?" Ted grunted. He was acting very natural, but I couldn't risk it being an act. I looked upon Ted as a friend, but when it comes to murder how friendly can you get?

"Enough money. Anybody in your office?"

"No. Why?"

"I need your help. Maybe I'll hire you."

"Can your client afford me? I charge too much to be padded into an expense account."

"That's what I want to talk over." I stopped the cabbie, paid him off. We walked down the block toward Ted's office. We passed a squad car stuck in the traffic. Ted didn't do anything. I had to test him but it was rough on my nerves. Main thing, he didn't know I was wanted.

Once in his office I said, "It's like this, Ted, I want to rent one of your bugs, get checked out on it. Kind I can carry around on me. I'll need a record of a conversation with a guy tonight."

Ted belched and rubbed his pot belly. "I don't know; if you lose the bug or bust it, runs into folding money. Besides, that isn't worth a bad dime as evidence, only your word against his. Better tell me what you got in mind, Toussaint."

"Will you rent the stuff to me or not?"

"Now don't get huffy. I been learning about this tape stuff, and I'm trying to help you. If you really want to nail down evidence, it's best to have two men listening in. What you got in mind?"

I suddenly changed my plans, took a deep breath and plunged in—trusting a white man with my life. "I'll level with you, Ted, I'm jammed up. I want you to do me two favors. I'm going to tell you something. If you don't like the way it sounds, forget I told you a word. If, after you hear me out, well, if you want to help me—that's the second favor." If Ted backed out it wouldn't be much of a fight tying him up for the night, then doing the obvious—beating the truth out of Steve.

"You mean I'll be a little accessory to something?" he said, smiling wisely.

"The something happens to be murder." The smile turned false and sickly, his whole face went gray. But since I had my feet wet I had to go in all the way. Ted listened as I told him everything that had happened from the second Kay walked into my office. I talked for a long time and when I was finished Ted took a cigar from a desk box, broke off a hunk and started chewing on it, thinking. I sat on the edge of his desk, right on top of him, watching and ready for any move he might make.

Finally he said in a weary voice, "All right, sit down, Toussaint, I'm not going to tangle with you. You got me on a hell of a spot. It'd be different if you hadn't slugged the cop. I don't have to tell you a private badge can't operate unless he keeps on the good side of the police, and helping a cop fighter—Geezoo!"

"Will you buy this: I came up here, slugged you, took a tape recorder and tied you up for the night?" I asked, wondering what difference it made if he agreed or not.

"I didn't say I was turning you down. I'm in. Can we see this Kay babe on the quiet and—?"

"Wait a minute, let's play open poker—why are you sticking your neck out for me?"

"Well," Ted grunted, "it ain't because I like you or any of that slop. I mean, friendship doesn't go for murder raps. If you knocked off Thomas I don't picture you hanging around New York, or telling me about it. So I got to go along with you being innocent. Toussaint, I'll level with you: that's an important contact you have and if we can break this my agency will be all over the papers and up and down Madison Avenue. It's worth the gamble."

"And if it turns out McDonald has nothing to do with anything?"

Ted rubbed his square hands together, as if drying them. "Then I'm messed up. I said it was a gamble—bet nothing, you win nothing. Now sit down and let's talk. I wish you'd come earlier; I could call a credit house* and get a complete rundown on McDonald, Kay, the others. But now I'll have to wait till tomorrow, and way I see it we have to act tonight. If the cops get us *before* we come up with anything—I'm too old to take a beating. We have to talk this Kay into helping us."

"Why her?" I asked, moving into a chair but still watching him, ready to jump on him. "I figured I'd see Steve, accuse him, and get everything down on tape. I don't trust Kay."

"But she's the only one who can give us any information on this stooge you mentioned. As for her being in on the murder, I can't see that. No motive. True, we don't know McDonald's motive either, but being a relative he can have a dozen motives we can't possibly know of. Also, if Kay was the big mind behind this, she wouldn't have had you up to her house to meet her friends. We have to talk her into going to McDonald's apartment

---

* Ted means an agency like Dun & Bradstreet, a source of credit reports and business investigations and evaluations.

tonight, or getting him up to her place. She plants a bug and we can be a block away in a car, getting it down. She'll come right out and accuse him of killing his cousin. Even if he didn't do it, I bet his answers will give us a lead, make damn interesting listening."

"If Steve's our boy, he'll knock her off, too."

"She gets him up to her apartment, we'll be in the next room, ready to take him. Nice, we have three witnesses to his story."

"Suppose Steve and Kay are in this together?"

"Naw, that doesn't figure. As I just said, if she had anything to do with this, she would have kept you a secret, not invited you up to see her friends. No, it has to be Kay, it even looks right. Being they were working on the same TV show, etcetera, she'd be the one to suspect him. Main point is, will she have the guts to work with us?"

"And if she turns us down?"

"We're in a bad way."

"I still think I should see him, plant a bug, and you be down in the car, recording what he says."

Bailey sent a stream of brown tobacco juice into the waste basket. "Toussaint, if he is the killer, and has set you up, why should he admit a thing to you? Been my experience that criminals like to brag, especially these one-shot amateurs. Talking is a form of confession for them, and he'd love to shoot off his trap in front of her."

"But they were lovey-dovey the last time I heard."

"If she's a career gal, she won't want to be playing house with a killer." He glanced at his watch. "Think she'll be home now? We can't risk phoning; we'll barge in. Faster we see her, the better; probably take a lot of talking to convince her she has to take a chance."

He got up and I jumped and he said, "Relax, Toussaint, this

ain't the time for jumpy nerves." He unlocked a cabinet, brought
out a tape recorder about the size of a portable typewriter, and
some other gadgets. "In this holster there's a Minifone recorder,*
with the mike on your wrist, like a watch. Now this,"—he held
up something the size of an old-fashioned pocket match box,
with a pin sticking out of it—"is a little broadcasting station.
You ought to see the inside; got transistors—that's like radio
tubes—big as beans and batteries no larger than a dime. It's
really something. My engineer showed it all to me once. You pin
this under a chair or on the back of a couch and it will broadcast
about 150 yards. Good for 30 hours."

"Looks like a toy," I said, examining the little box. Didn't
weigh more than a box of matches either.

"Don't juggle it; my heart can't take the strain. If you knew
what these 'toys' cost…I keep telling you this racket has become
for engineers. I buy 'em, but you think I know what it's all about?
My engineer showed me enough so I can work 'em, that's all I
need to know. Ready?"

"Yeah," I said, feeling like an ingrate. I didn't like Ted's plan
but couldn't think of anything better.

As he dropped his gray Homburg on his head, Ted said,
"There's one condition, Toussaint. If we should be stopped by
the cops, don't run for it or put up a fight. You'll have to let them
take you in, trust they believe your story. I don't think they'll
even start to believe it, but—I'm willing to gamble, but not with
my life. Carrying a gun?"

"No."

---

* Actually the brand name was Minifon, and the device, introduced in 1951, was widely
advertised as "the world's smallest recorder" and was popular with spy agencies as well
as private investigators. It was developed by a German engineer, Willi Draheim, and
was first marketed for commercial use as an expensive "Dictaphone" (a popular brand
of dictation machine) for making an accurate record of a conversation. A "p.55" model
cost $350 in 1955.

He bent over the small office safe, opened it, and took out two guns. I said, "I never even applied for a permit."

Ted grunted softly. "Nuts. With what we're stepping into, a Sullivan Law* rap won't matter much. Since I have a permit, let me carry both rods until we go into action."

For a fearful second, as he was busy locking the safe up, I had the feeling I was trapped. But I kept telling myself he would have thrown a gun on me right now if he was crossing me.

As he opened the door and turned out the lights, I stepped into the hallway. Ted said, "I know what you're thinking. Sure, I'd get some publicity for turning you in. But what would it prove, except I was lucky because you dropped in to see me? Who would I be selling, the police? Don't worry, Toussaint, I'm not a rat nor a noble character....I'm in this simply to convince Madison Avenue what a hot investigator I am—not police headquarters. We understand each other?"

"Perfectly," I said, trying to believe him.

Ted kept his '53 Buick in a nearby garage and I carried the recorder as we walked to the car. At first I was a little steamed, his telling me to carry it like I was his servant or something, but I calmed down when I realized it was almost a form of disguise on the street—as though I was a part of the routine of the city.

We kept circling Kay's block, looking for a place to park. When I asked why he passed up a spot on Third Avenue, Ted said, "Too far. Just in case we decide to do the recording in the car, I want it ready to pick up the bug. That means not more than a block away, or less."

As we were turning into her block, on our tenth lap, a Caddy pulled out across the street from Kay's house. Before we could get there, a New Jersey car stopped and started to back in as Ted

---

* A gun control act that took effect in 1911 in New York.

cursed. I ran over and flashed my badge fast, said, "Police. Park elsewhere, we need this spot."

A thin guy in a tux was behind the wheel and he rubbed his sharp nose with one finger as he repeated, "Police?"

"Didn't you see the badge?" I asked, a growl in my voice. "Come on, get going."

"Well....Yes sir, officer. I always co-operate with the police. Raiding somebody?"

"Don't ask questions about police business."

"Of course, you're right," he said, driving away. Ted parked and got out, locking the car. The New Jersey guy was waiting at the corner for a light, looking back at us. It was okay, we looked like detectives, burly, and Ted dressed like one. I told Ted to wait. When the guy finally turned the corner, we crossed over to her house, rang her bell. When the door buzzed open I said, "Two of us can't fit in this elevator. I'll walk up, you give me a minute's head start."

"Good, but wait until I get there before you show yourself."

I sprinted up the cement stairs, then waited, panting, until the elevator came and Ted stepped out. He walked over to the door, held his gold shield against the peephole and said, "Detective."

As the door opened he pushed in and I ran in behind him, shut the door. Wearing a pale blue Chinese housecoat over a slip, Kay was standing by the door. Barbara was sitting at a table set for supper, an apron over her gray-knit sheath dress.

They both screamed: small yells of fear and surprise. Then Kay wailed, "Touie, they have you!" That was a confusing sound too, sort of a hysterical sigh.

Bobby jumped to her feet, ready to scream again, or burst into tears. Ted said, "Now ladies, things will be fine if you'll relax, no screams, don't run to the phone or—"

I cut in with, "This is Ted Bailey, a friend of mine. He's a private detective."

The real relief I saw on both their faces was a shot in the arm—neither Kay nor Bobby had blown the whistle on me. Kay hugged me. "I've been so worried about you, Touie. I felt at fault for involving you in all this."

I held her for a moment, asked, "You two alone?"

"Yes. Oh Touie, are you all right?"

"I don't know," I said, pushing her away—gently. "The police been asking about me?"

"No."

"No?"

"Of course, when we read about the murder the office was thrown into a first-rate gasser.* It was immediately agreed to drop the Thomas story from *You—Detective!* Then—"

"Kay, you mean Central hasn't told the police about me?"

Kay gave me her tight smile. "Of course not. Very few people knew of the publicity stunt, and in view of the murder any news of it would now be in extremely poor taste. Of course we had no way of knowing what you would say, and that had us worried. Naturally I discussed it with B.H. He had a chat with a member of Central's legal staff who happens to be a personal friend of somebody high up in the police department. In an off-the-cuff talk with the police, our lawyer was told the police knew all about you, that is, knew your identity. It was agreed Central would be kept out of the case as far as possible."

"How would Central be kept out? By making sure a trigger-happy cop killed me if I should be collared!"

"Don't be nasty, Touie. We decided that if you were caught, we would see you had the best lawyers. There would be a slight

---

* A "gasser" is something wonderful or exceptional. *Partridge*, 843.

change in our story, something you couldn't possibly object to: I had hired you merely to recheck the facts on Thomas. After all, you can't blame Central—they have millions invested in their network."

Their millions and shame on this brown boy! I thought.

Kay smiled again. "I wouldn't let them throw you to the dogs. This way we'd covered ourselves and it turned out fine. The police weren't too interested in you or—"

"I don't get this about the cops," Ted cut in.

"The cops aren't interested *in* me, only in framing me into the electric chair!" I got it all right: if I said anything about the publicity deal, Central would claim I was nuts.

"There!" Bobby said, as if making a profound statement. "I told Kay you didn't do it."

Kay waved a slim hand in the air. "Now I never said—My God, what did happen in that room, Touie?"

"A setup. Somebody claiming they were you phoned my office, left a message I was to be in Thomas' room at midnight. He was dead when I got there. Moment later a cop came busting in."

"Claiming I was calling?" Kay began. "I don't see how any-body could know—"

"That's what I'm here for, to find the answers to a few questions. I'm still under the frame. Two things I want to know. You said after the Thomas case was televised, you—Central—had a stooge set to turn him in to the police. Who is the stooge?"

"Because of the secrecy, we hadn't told the—eh—stooge yet. There's a pensioned watchman who worked for Central we planned to hire. Either he or his wife, they could use the money."

"Okay, we'll forget that angle. Now, what's playing between you and Steve McDonald?"

Kay flushed. "What has my—?"

"There's nothing between them!" Bobby said loudly, rushing over to place a protective arm around Kay. "She was home the next morning. She's finished with him."

Kay broke away from Bobby, took her pipe out of a pocket in the Chinese coat, calmly lit it as Ted's eyes got large. "I really don't see what my personal affairs have to do with all this, Touie."

"Kay, I'm not asking to keep up with the local gossip. I have a damn good reason."

Kay blew a whiff of smoke at me. "I'm smoking that brand you recommended. About Steve, it isn't worth talking about. I admit, I was silly. Steve isn't anything...a...caterpillar. So terribly dull that actually all that happened was I got very drunk at his place."

"And passed out?"

"How did you know? We started out late in the afternoon and he acted so cocky, and over nothing, why, it became boring. I drank too much, did a loop-the-loop early in the evening. Now that I've confessed my all, I still don't get the bit about Steve."

"He is—or was—Thomas' cousin."

"Honest?" Kay asked, as if we were playing kid games.

I nodded.

Kay chuckled as she dropped on the couch. "Oh, this is simply priceless. His cousin! And the way the smug bastard ate up the white-haired wonder-boy role. This explains how he was able to come up with a complete script on Thomas overnight. It was his speed that nailed down the writing assignment for the rest of the scripts and—"

"Did McDonald know about your publicity idea?" Ted cut in.

Kay gave him a long look. "I see you do, too." Then she sent an accusing glance at me.

"For the love of Mike,* Kay, snap out of it. Sure I told Ted. What about Steve, was he in on things?"

She ran a hand over her cropped copper hair, as if fitting it on her head. "The morning after I hired you, when I was telling B.H. about it, long distance, he suggested letting Steve in on it. He seemed such a buster of an idea boy we thought he might come up with—God, you think he did it?"

"I don't know, but I'm going to find out tonight—if you'll help me."

"What's Kay got to do with this?" Bobby asked. "I'm certainly not going to chance her getting hurt or involved in—"

"Be still, Butch. What is it you want me to do?"

I told her what we had in mind and Ted added, "You see, Miss, he'll shoot off his mouth to you, to a girl. Me or Toussaint confronted him he'd clam up. If we beat it out of him, it wouldn't stand up in court."

Kay touched her hair again, nodding as she puffed on her pipe. She seemed only interested in watching the smoke going up toward the ceiling. Bobby said, "Surely you aren't asking Kay to risk her neck with a murderer!"

"Ted and I will be in the next room. We'll take care of Steve before he can do—"

Kay went through the slim hand-waving routine again. "Now shut up, the two of you. I want to think. It has its points. Trouble is, if I'm involved the publicity angle might come to light. That would be disastrous for the network."

"The hell with the network, my life is at stake!"

Kay showed me her tight little smile once more. "Touie, I realize that, but don't be melodramatic. Career is another word for life and my career is at stake."

---

* A euphemism for "for the love of God" or "for the love of Jesus." *Partridge*, 788.

"Kay is right," Bobby said. "Suppose Steve isn't the killer, or won't admit a thing, where does that leave Kay?"

Kay shook her head. "Bobby, I'm not worrying about that cockroach. No, suppose he *is* the murderer, where does that leave Central and the show?"

"Damn you, Kay, this is murder, not a goddamn show!" I said, trying not to shout.

Like somebody in a hammy play, she puffed on her pipe for a moment, and the silence in the room seemed ready to explode. Then she stood up. "I'm going to chance it!"

"Oh, Kay," Bobby said.

"I'm counting on the sponsor being a crime fan, that he'll buy it. The way I see all this, assuming Steve is our boy, we switch the Thomas sequence to the opening show—we'll be all over the papers for the next eight days. I'll see to that. We open to nation-wide headline publicity. The show will be watched by everybody in the country. Yes! Bobby, you know I have a special sense about publicity, and this hits me exactly right. A natural. Of course the publicity angle can't be exposed....Touie was merely hired to check on Tutt really being Thomas. Don't you see it? A show which caused a Central writer to murder...and the network boldly solves it, cleans its own house in the name of law and order. This can't miss!" Her voice actually came alive, full of excitement.

"Now Kay honey," Barbara said, "hadn't you better check with B.H. first? Call him and—"

"No, no," I cut in. "No phoning anybody. If McDonald is warned I'm sunk."

Barbara said, "You don't think we'd—?"

"Look, for all I know B.H. can be the killer, or in on it with McDonald."

Kay said, "Stop all the talk. I'm not calling B.H. I'm doing this solely on my responsibility. It'll amount to more if I pull it off."

"Sure, it will amount to my life—if anybody is interested in that besides me," I said.

"Oh stop the self-pity," Kay told me. "Now what is it you want me to do—in detail?"

Ted said, "First off, can you hire my agency? Officially. I want to be in on this."

"Damn it," I said, boiling over, "give her the pitch some other time. Now listen, here's the deal." I told her about the bug and the recorder and getting Steve up to her place. When I finished Kay didn't hesitate a second to say, "Fine I'll phone Steve right now."

But Bobby got to the phone first. "Kay, why can't I be the one? He knows I'm familiar with all the details of the publicity project, so it would be logical for me to suspect him."

"That's terribly sweet and brave of you, Bobby-boy, but you see it has to be me because I'm representing Central in all this mess. I'll phone him now, hint something has come up concerning the studio—that should bring him on the run. How soon should I tell him to come?"

"Right away," I said. "There's one more piece of business before we start. I've socked a cop. Now, if we pin anything on Steve, I want you three to stick with me all the time I'm with the cops, even at the precinct house. I'm not going for any beating."

"Don't worry," Ted told me blandly, "we give them the real killer and they'll be happy."

"Maybe, but I want you around for insurance."

"Touie is right. We all know why the cops may want to beat him up, and I have a better idea," Kay said, knocking the ashes out of her jeweled pipe. "Let me phone a reporter friend, have him stand by. If we get anything on Steve, we'll phone the reporter before calling the police. Publicity wise it will be fine, because this fellow works for one of the big wire services. Okay, Touie?"

I nodded and she dialed some guy and, after the small talk and assuring him this wasn't merely another news plant or publicity release, he agreed to wait for her call. We were wasting time and I had her call Steve, the tenseness inside me coiling tighter with each turn of her phone dial. After a moment Kay hung up, said there wasn't any answer. The letdown must have shown on my face; she said, "He's probably out for supper, Touie. It isn't seven yet. I suggest we finish eating. Hungry, Mr. Bailey?"

Matter of fact, I was starving, and damn if we all didn't have supper as though we were waiting to go on a party instead of hooking a killer. Kay kept trying Steve's number every fifteen minutes, and in the meantime we had to watch TV. Kay wanted to "catch" certain shows and commercials. Ted phoned his wife to tell her he was working, and then he sat and stared at Bobby and Kay, his eyes bewildered. I had the same feeling I had in Bingston hanging around the Davis house: I began to wonder if all this was real or a nightmare.

Ted went down to check his car, kept worrying somebody would steal the equipment. Bobby had a kettle boiling in the fireplace and served hot rums. By ten I was a jumpy wreck, certain Steve had flown the coop. Kay was sipping too many rums and I snapped, "Don't get crocked."

"I'm too excited for that. But I do need a few belts from the bottle of courage, as the non-A.A.* people romantically call it. Rum doesn't relax Bobby. Butch, you look tired, why don't you take a sleep pill?"

At five to eleven she finally got Steve, and I almost melted away with relief. Kay asked, "Steve, can you come up to my place at once? What? Don't be an ass, not if you were the last pair of pants in the universe. This is strictly business. I've found

---

* Alcoholics Anonymous.

out something at the office that will make you drool. Oh, don't hand me any creative-mood junk. You can write later: this is important. No, no, I can't discuss it on the phone. Okay, stay with your typewriter, Hemingway." She winked at us over the receiver. "But I have the inside dope on a new show—biggest thing in your career—a full net series, twice a week. Oh, I'm not kidding. You'll have to get on your horse and bring in a sample outline by tomorrow afternoon. Bighearted? Listen, I want a straight twenty per cent cut if you land the scripting....I don't see why you can't come over. What? I'm offering you a big deal on a silver platter and you're playing coy...."

I tapped her shoulder, said in pantomime, "Tell him you'll go to his place."

She nodded. "Steve, this is really big; suppose I come up to see you. You're damn right I'm money-hungry...when it's upper-bracket money. I'll be over within the hour. I have to dress and—All right, all right, cut the sex talk. I'm serious. I'll be up soon as I can."

As she hung up Bobby cried, "Kay, don't, don't!"

"Oh Bobby, relax. Take your pill and go to sleep."

"No! I won't let you go alone!"

I said, "You can't go with Kay—louse up everything."

"I insist. I won't let Kay face that creature alone!"

Ted said, "Since we'll have to do the tape in the car, let her stay downstairs with me. Another witness won't hurt." He pulled the matchbox transmitter from his pocket, showed it to Kay. "This is important, so listen. You carry this in your bag, and make sure it don't get stuck to the bag. You have to play this smart and careful; if he sees it we're sunk. When you sit down, pin this under a chair, or on the back of a couch—anyplace where it isn't covered up and can't be seen. And you got to do it soon as you get inside his apartment."

Kay poked a finger at the box. "This tiny gadget really broadcasts?"

"Yeah, I'll set it soon as you're ready. And be careful with it. It costs like crazy, too."

Kay pinched the Chinese robe, said almost to herself, "I ought to get into a bitchy dress—something real seductive."

"Kay!" Bobby said.

"My God, the very last thing I want is Steve McDonald. I'll be a moment." She went into the bedroom.

I called after her, "What sort of house does he live in?"

"One of these remodeled deals, but larger than this house."

"Sport a doorman?"

"No, I don't think so."

"Does he live on the front or back?"

"I don't remember. He has one large room and kitchenette. Fantastically decorated."

"Is it on a fire escape?"

"Really, how would I know?"

Ted and I got our coats while Bobby slipped into a tailored cloth coat and bebop cap,* which didn't look at all mannish on her. Kay walked in wearing spike heels and a light silver strapless gown with a built-in shelf bra that served up her small breasts. Her face wasn't made up, the copper-colored hair carefully— but casually—brushed around her head. The gown and hair set off her thin shoulders and all of it added up to sex. Tossing a mink cape on her shoulders she said, "Now I'm prepared. I always said I'd wear this mink till the day I died."

"Kay, please!" Bobby whined.

Ted held up his thick hands. "Let's get things straight. I'll let you women out on the corner, in case this McDonald is the

---

* A flat newsboy cap.

suspicious type and looking out his window. When we find a parking space, Bobby here will walk down to the car. Kay, you wait in front of McDonald's house for Toussaint, who will go up and get on the fire escape, be set before you enter the apartment. That may not be easy." He glanced at me and we were both thinking the same thing: a Negro seen on the roof or fire escape in a white neighborhood would bring a dozen frantic calls to the police. "If a fire escape is out, I think Toussaint should plant himself outside McDonald's door, batter it down when the time comes."

"How can I hear through a door?" I asked. Loitering in a hallway would be dangerous as the devil—for me.

"Planned that," Ted grunted. "It's late and quiet out. Soon as Kay plants the bug, I'll give three short blasts of the car horn—meaning the bug is sending okay. If it ain't working, if you don't hear the horn within five minutes after you set the bug, get the bug back and leave. You tell him, Kay, you have a headache or—"

"It has to be tonight," I cut in.

"The main thing is it has to be done right," Ted went on. "You don't hear the horn—here, better yet. If I'm not receiving, Bobby will phone; that will give Kay an excuse to leave. Now, if things go okay, I'm hearing everything, I'll give another three blasts of the horn if Kay seems in danger. Toussaint can then come through the door or window, and I'll be on my way up."

"That sounds good," Kay said.

"If Touie can't be outside a window, we can't go through with it," Bobby said. "It'd only take Steve a second to do...something."

Ted shook his big head. "Don't worry, ma'am. Once he hears somebody at the door, he'll only be doing one thing—trying to get out of there. And Toussaint will be armed."

"I can handle Steve. I've kicked a few men in the right place before," Kay said. "Let's go."

Bobby and Ted went down first while Kay and I waited for the elevator. "Are you nervous, Touie?" she asked calmly.

"Wish I knew more about the location of his apartment in the building."

"It's a walk-up and he's on the third floor, but that's all I remember. I'm really sorry I got you into this mess."

I shrugged. "Risks of the job, I guess."

Steve lived in the Sixties, east of Madison Avenue. Ted gave Kay the transmitter, making sure it was working, and she slipped it into her bag as she and Bobby got off at the corner. Ted said, "Now watch yourself, don't leave your bag when you take off your cape."

We turned into Sixty-fifth Street, which was empty of people but full of cars. There was only one open space, in front of a large apartment house, with NO PARKING lettered across the curb. I told Ted to park there and he said the doorman would raise hell. I told him to park.

This old man dressed like a foreign general came rushing out and before he could say a word I shook his hand, said, "It's important we park here for about a half hour."

"You can't—" He saw the ten bucks I'd palmed in his hand, added, "Raise the hood of your car, like you're broken down. Only a half hour. What's this all about?"

"Divorce raid.* Not in your house." We were in a good spot, on the same side of the street and less than a hundred feet from Steve's place.

I raised the hood as Ted fooled with the tape recorder. Then I stepped into the shadow of the nearest building. Bobby came down the block first, got into the car, while the old doorman stood in the doorway of the building, watched us with

---

* Not an uncommon activity for private detectives in New York—gathering evidence of adultery as grounds for a divorce.

suspicious eyes. As Kay walked toward the house, I walked up the street, stepped into the small lobby of Steve's house right behind her. I said, "No fire escape on the front. Ring the bell and walk up. Wait at least ten minutes before you put the question to him, but hook up the bug soon as you can. Understand?"

She nodded and rang his bell, apartment 3D. When he buzzed the door open we both stepped inside and she walked up. I stood in the hallway, wondering what I'd do if anybody came in, asked what I was doing there, or gave me one of those *looks*, which would be the same as a question. There was more than an even chance the moment they reached a phone they'd call the police: "There's a burly Negro in the lobby of..."

I heard Steve open the door, say something impatiently, then the silence of the house again as he closed the door. I waited a second, then went up the stairs, moving softly, almost walking in slow motion. Passing the second floor I saw the "D" apartments were in the rear, on the left side. The halls were fireproofed, with a window at the rear of the hall—must be a fire escape there. When I reached the roof, sweating heavily, I lit a match. The door looked okay, no Holmes alarm.* I unlocked it and stepped out into the cool air, my darkness swallowed in the black of night.

I shut my eyes, then opened them slowly, looked around at the cemetery of TV aerials like weird crosses. It was simple. An iron ladder went down the back of the roof to the fire escape. There was a small rear yard and then the back of other houses, lights showing in many rooms. There was only one fire escape.

---

* Edwin Holmes did not invent the burglar alarm, but in the mid-nineteenth century, he was the most successful marketer of alarm systems in the United States, promoting the "Holmes Burglar Alarm Telegraph." His success may be marked by the number of real estate advertisements in which the presence of one of his devices was touted as a selling point. Holmes's companies dominated the industry for years, and as can be seen, a "Holmes" alarm became essentially a generic term for a burglar alarm system.

They must have smeared an inspector to get away with it. Taking off my shoes and tying them around my neck, I started down the ladder. Passing the top hall window I was silhouetted like a target. Target…I'd forgotten something…Ted's gun.

9

I never had much use for pistols; the war had taught me to love a carbine. Still I felt kind of naked without Ted's pistol right now, and if I couldn't get the window open a hunk of lead could. So shame on me for being stupid and it was too late to worry about it.

In its tenement days there must have been two railroad flats to each floor, with front and rear entrances. These had been broken up into four large one-room apartments, and the two in the rear had wide windows on either side of the fire escape. The light was on in one of the top-floor apartments and I saw a man sprawled on a couch, reading a paper, as I went down the roof ladder to the fire escape. That didn't worry me: unless a person was looking directly out at the fire escape, and that meant looking through the window at an angle, I was safe. What made me nervous was passing the lighted hall window on each floor—anybody glancing out of a window across the back yard would have to see me.

On the fourth floor a dog barked as I went down the iron steps, which felt like ice through my woolen socks. Happily the mutt let it go at one bark and on the third floor I got another break: Steve's light was on, of course, but the apartment on the other side of the fire escape was dark, the window opened slightly for air. Steve had an air-conditioning unit sticking out of the bottom half of his window. Leaving my shoes on the steps I got up on the railing, hoped the air-conditioning box would hold me as I faced the building and tried to get a grip on the rough brick with my big fingers. I put one foot out on the air-conditioning box. It seemed pretty firm. With the other foot on the fire-escape railing I was okay—if I hadn't been seen from across the back yard—lost in the shadows outside the hall window. I had a fair view of his room and the window wasn't locked. I could open the window and step right into the room.

The room was something out of the 1890's. The wallpaper was a mess of big roses and little cupids dancing around, the chandelier was a clumsy affair of cut glass, the furniture was all stuffed plush and leather chairs, with a narrow four-poster bed in one corner. Even the pictures had old heavy gold frames and on the tables and bookcases I saw old bric-a-brac vases and china. I don't know, it was so obviously affected it stank.

Steve was wearing a red satin smoking jacket, a cigarette dangling from his thin lips. Kay was sitting in what seemed like half a chaise longue, lying back on it, her feet on the floor, the tops of her stockings showing. The chaise was made of a horrible cream yellow and damn if the transmitter wasn't hanging from the bottom of it, under the slight curve her backside made. Her skirt neatly hid it from Steve. She seemed completely at ease. I had to admire her for being real cool when it counted.

With different furniture it would have been a nice apartment; the room was large, and through two open doors I saw the john and a small kitchenette. There seemed to be a window in the kitchen, probably opened on an air shaft. By stretching my neck I could see an old-fashioned roll-top desk, opened, a typewriter and stacks of manuscript. Next to the desk stood a small marble top table with gold legs, holding up a couple of bottles and an ice bucket, and a huge milk-glass lamp. I could hear them talking and they were both calm. Steve asked if she wanted a drink and Kay said no. Then he asked if it was true about some dame who was said to be living with one of Central's vice-presidents and Kay said that was old hat.

The bottom of my feet were numb with cold, my hands ached from holding on to the brick wall—and I suddenly felt blue, real lousy blue. The whole deal seemed ridiculous—what would a nut like Steve have to do with a murder? Why should these two white people help me? Here I was, standing spread-eagled, expecting a slug in the back any minute, a killing fall under me. I had this terrible feeling I was wasting time, that it was all helpless, I was doomed.

The three horn blasts from the street made me snap out of it. The bug was sending okay. Steve held his ears. "That god-damn bastard! Every morning around eight some jerk honks his horn, too lazy to get out and ring a bell. Wonder a cop doesn't give him a ticket. By God, if I had a front apartment, I'd toss a bottle down on him. Grates my nerves." He shook himself to show how it all grated. "Well, darling, what's the big deal you're in an uproar about?"

"My, my, aren't we impatient now," she said coyly. "When I phoned you acted as if you couldn't care less."

"That wasn't it. I'm finishing the tenth script for *You—Detective!* and once the juices start flowing I dislike being disturbed. What's the big flash?"

She even smiled as she said, "I've been thinking about the killing of Tutt…Thomas."

Steve flicked his cigarette ashes into a glass. "What kind of a show can be made out of that?"

"That's what I'm asking you," Kay said softly, staring up at him. "Came to me that only three people knew about the publicity angle on Thomas—myself, B.H., and you."

Steve was a cool one too. "And one more—that private eye you hired. The black eye, if you'll excuse the pun, or did I crack that once before? What has the publicity stunt to do with Thomas' death?"

"I don't know, but it hit me that maybe it has some connection. That's why I was thinking about Thomas—although the police think Touie did it, what possible motive could he have?"

Steve made his eyes big. "Dear, if you've cut into my work just to play detective...Who knows why Moore did it? Perhaps Thomas caught him snooping and put up a fight. In a moment of anger anything can happen."

"What can happen in a moment of truth?"

"Darling, you're far too deep for me tonight. What's this all about?"

"That fight bit doesn't fit, Steve. That's been worrying me because I told Touie he didn't have to keep a tight tab on Thomas until after the program was aired, so..."

"Kay, have you heard from your Othello?"

"Of course not, but I suppose we're all detectives at heart, so I've been doing some thinking about it tonight. Certainly B.H. didn't have a reason to kill Thomas; he wasn't even in town. I know I didn't."

The big eyes again, mocking her. "And then there was one little Indian left...me?"

She giggled. "It did seem odd he should be killed on the very day you were let in on the publicity secret."

Steve laughed, real deep laughter. "Darling, if you're looking for an excuse to try it in bed again, don't be so clumsy. In fact, maybe we should make love—you're priceless tonight. You're simply hysterical when you're in heat and trying to—"

"B.H. seems to share my idea."

"Bull." It came out like the snap of a small whip. "I had a chat with him this afternoon; I would have known if he had anything on his alleged mind. No, Kay, this is a woman's trick, and poorly done. You're sore because we didn't make it in the hay, and trying to take it out on me with this wild accusation. You need couch time with a competent headshrinker. Lord, why should I kill Tutt? He was the best break I've ever had."

"Exactly, Steve. I remembered how you came up with a script on Thomas overnight. How did you do the research so quickly? The local newspaper morgues would be useless."

"All women have lousy memories. Did you forget that I had a similar show in mind, that I'd already done a rough audition script on Tutt?" He flashed his big eyes at her again, as if proving something.

My right foot was so numb I shifted my weight slightly to the foot resting on the fire-escape railing. When I put weight back on the right foot the damn air-conditioning box groaned and my heart froze.

But Steve was too steamed to hear it. "I don't mind a gag. However I resent this ridiculous accusation, this scummy knife in the back. Now get out of here! I warn you, any whisper of this around the studio and I'll be forced to tell them the truth."

"What's the truth?"

"Now darling, dumbness doesn't become you. I can tell them how you grew tired of your Bobby and tried going with me, but you're in a rage to realize you're so much a Lesbian now you can't have a normal relationship with a man."

She thumbed her nose at him. "Now that would be a

delightful booboo. Everybody knows you're as queer as an icicle in hell, a fruit who—"

"You didn't think so!" he said, lighting another cigarette. "Look, Kay, let's be adult. There's no point in kicking each other. I'm busy. Tomorrow I'll even buy you lunch and we can continue going along with the gag." Then he popped his eyes, added, "By the bye, I left out one part of my little booboo, as you quaintly called it—a part Madison Avenue won't think cute. You see I might add that one of the reasons you went with me was that that black boy wouldn't give you a tumble."

"Maybe he gave me a real tumble, that's why I wasn't content with your nance pawing."

"Did he bring you down some Harlem reefers too? Are you on tea now? Are you on a sadistic kick? Because if you are, I'm in the mood to accommodate you with a very fine beating, my dear."

"Stevie, don't make a speech. I did more than kick this around in my bird brain...I made a few calls to Kentucky."

I could feel the heavy silence of the room out on the fire escape; then he split it with a thin scream. "You bitch!" His long thin face flushed a deep pink, then went deadly white.

Kay didn't even jump; she was enjoying this. She made her tight smile, then said, "My, that cut through the veneer of coolness, didn't it? Now suppose you cut the dramatics and in basic English tell me about Cousin Thomas."

He didn't say a word, stood there very straight, his face a mixture of pain and anger.

She put the knife in deeper, turned it. "Stevie, you don't understand the bit. I'm giving you a break. For the sake of the show I'm giving you a chance to talk to me—before I talk to the police."

"How...how...did you find out?" His voice was in hoarse pieces now.

"It's too late for how. You're always so glib, do some fast talking now. Why did you kill him?"

He fell back against a table, seemed actually to shrink and wrinkle up. Then he pulled himself together, took a deep breath, and was under control again. Even made his big eyes as he walked over and sat on the edge of his desk, relit his cigarette. "Of course I'll talk—it's a story you can understand. I killed him. But wait till—"

There was another scream, a tiny muffled scream of joy and relief that stayed in my throat.

"—you hear it all. It wasn't murder. Thomas is a distant cousin of mine, the family black sheep, our skeleton in the closet. He was a lump, his mother a common slut. You see my situation; I wrote my novel and nothing happened. I *had* to make it as a writer or be stuck in a goddamn hick store the rest of my life, a drunken failure. I gassed around Hollywood for a time, couldn't get in. I returned to New York and tried TV. I worked like a dog. For two lousy years I wrote on spec, was in on a dozen package deals that ended in nothing. I was desperate—for Christsakes I'm thirty-six years old. I can't keep asking my sick Dad for eating money!"

"And then you heard about *You—Detective!*" Kay added, reaching over to the table for one of his cigarettes.

He lit it for her as he said, "I'd been sucking around Central for a long time. This was my *in*. While I'd only seen Porky a few—"

"Porky?"

"Bob Thomas' nickname. He had the manners of a pig, I suppose. As I was saying, I'd only seen him a few times when we were kids, but family gossip gave me a rundown of his crimes. Frankly, I'd forgotten all about him until I saw him in Times Square, going to work. I didn't let him see me. It would only have meant a touch. I was thinking of doing a fast paperback on him...when I heard about the show. It was a snap for me to bat out a script during the night. It worked, flung the doors wide open for me....Suddenly I was a success boy. The world was bright and sunny. I figured there was little chance of Porky being caught as a result of the show. It would be forgotten with the next twist of the dial. Anyway, he was a nobody, didn't matter. Sooner or later he'd end up in jail again. It was perfect for me."

Kay nodded, puffing on her cigarette slowly. She either was a fine actress or actually thought all this was the most normal thinking in the world.

Steve crushed his cigarette and lit another—all in one practiced motion. "When you told me Porky had been picked for the publicity bit, I panicked. Offhand, the chances were a thousand to one that he'd even see the show, much less catch the titles—see my name. But once he was arrested, all the publicity and news stories, well, he'd *have* to know about me. He had nothing to lose. He'd be angry, and he'd most certainly tell of our family relationship. My TV career would have been kaput. I went down to see him that night, told him what the play was, offered him five hundred dollars to take a powder. He blew his lid, there was a fight....Then I was holding a bloody pair of pliers in my hand and he was dead. If I hadn't killed him, he would have done me in."

"Self-defense," Kay said, almost sympathetically.

"Obviously. Of course now there would certainly be a scandal and...I don't have to repeat the old saw about the law of survival. I had to think damn fast. I went out and disguising my voice phoned your black dick, said I was you. A simple thing; I've done a little acting. Had a bad moment when he wasn't home, but whoever answered was positive he could contact Moore. The rest was a matter of timing, phoning the police the moment I saw Moore enter the house. I was watching from a corner store. For what it's worth, I didn't enjoy it, but he fitted so nicely into things, and I had little choice. What the devil, I had my life's work in the balance, he would get a few years for manslaughter. What's a few years out of a nigger's life? So, now you have my story, the final installment, all up to date, my sweet."

"Aha."

He stood up, made his comical big eyes. "I'm sorry it has to be this way, Kay, because you're a lot of mixed-up fun. I sincerely mean that. And of course, it means getting in deeper, but again, I have no choice. Every action has a reaction—I have to kill you."

"I'm glad you said you did a *little* acting; you enjoy hammy dramatics, Stevie."

I heard three nervous blasts of the horn from the other side of the house.

He shrugged. "Dear, don't give me the business about I can trust you, that you'll never, never talk. I can't trust you."

"You're so right." Kay was terrific, not even a nervous twinge. Steve stepped out of character; like any other street-corner punk he whipped a large switch blade from his back pocket like an expert, the knife snapping open with the motion.

Kay's eyes were on the knife, but she still seemed to be enjoying things. He said, "As you know, I've never lacked ideas. This will fit: we had an unsatisfactory affair, which I'm sure isn't exactly a secret around the office, and now you've come up for another try. Certainly dressed for it. Again it didn't come off, you feel it's your fault, upset. I shall get drunk and pass out while you take an overdose of sleeping pills. Messy headlines, but otherwise safe."

I started to go into action, but Kay's calm voice asking, "That cheese sticker is going to make me do all this?" held me back. She seemed so cool, as if she hadn't finished playing out her role.

Steve nodded. "Come, my sweet, you're aware of the many... eh...parts...of a woman that can be slashed. I'm offering you a painless out. I can change the script—you slashed yourself before taking the pills. Fits in with the suicide bit."

"Stevie, you should have stayed at poppa's crossroads store; you're still a hick. This is all on tape. The joint *is* surrounded by detectives."

He laughed, short shrill laughter. "You can come up with better than that, Kay. I thought you were going to bluff me with a gun-in-my-bag routine."

"Steve, drop that knife, you're only making matters worse for yourself. There's a tiny transmitter pinned to the bottom of this chair. I placed it there myself. Look." She raised and opened her legs—a flash of silver skirt and stockinged thighs—so the bug was visible.

I stepped off the fire-escape railing. With my full weight on the air-conditioning box for a second, it started to sag. I felt myself going backward. With a frantic lunge, hands in front of my face, I pitched forward, crashing through the window. I hit the floor with a thud that jarred me dizzy, cut in a dozen places.

Shrieking, Steve turned and charged at me. I rolled over, jumped to my feet, slipping in my blood. I feinted with my right. He slashed at the forearm—I was cut in so many places I didn't know if he'd nicked me or not. I had a solid left winging toward his gut. It landed high, on his chest, and he stood stock-still, then crumpled to the floor.

"Are you all right?" I asked Kay. She nodded and I said, "You heard his confession. Of course that...self-defense is crap. Thomas's blood was still wet when I got there....Steve killed him *after* he phoned me. Probably stunned him, then finished him when—Where are you going?" Outside I could hear Ted pounding up the stairs.

Kay was at the phone. "Calling that reporter before—Touie, look out!"

Steve, this skinny, rugged slob, was back on his feet, without the knife. As I turned to face him this bag of bones nailed me on the chin with a wild right that sent my legs into a rubbery dance. If he'd clouted me again I might have gone out. Instead, he came at me, clawing, knees digging into my thighs. I put my arms around him in a bear hug and squeezed. His face went sallow white, the eyes really popped. When I let go he slid to the floor—no trouble for a lot of minutes.

Either because of the punch, or from loss of blood, after that things moved fast and jerky, like in an old-time movie. Ted and Bobby came busting in when I finally got the door unlocked—and Ted's two-pants suit seemed the only real thing in sight, somehow made me think of that farm back in Bingston.

In a matter of seconds, or so it seemed, there were a fat reporter and a young kid photographer, and a dozen cops filled up the room. I was getting blood over one of Steve's plush chairs, trying to answer a million questions and not saying anything clearly. Finally I simply sat there and watched the others talking and rushing about. A little runty ambulance doc appeared and ripped off what remained of my clothes, gave me a shot of something that left me hovering in midair. I knew he was cleaning my cuts, stitching here and there, and then I was insisting I could stand okay and a cop gave me a blanket to wear.

Maybe I dozed. Now we were in the local precinct house, with the police brass and more reporters, flash bulbs going off in salvos. Steve must have decided to go for insane; he was gibbering and screaming until they carried him out of the room. I was watching things like a spectator, but two things I remember clearly.

Kay—the photographers had a holiday with her dress and breastworks—was the busiest person in the police station, but she got me off in a corner and shoved a piece of paper and a pen in my bandaged hands, said, "Sign this, Touie. We're going to re-enact everything on film, to show after *You—Detective!* premières with the Thomas episode. Lord, Lord, there never will be a publicity splash like this! I couldn't do more with a million-dollar budget...it's a river and I'm squeezing every drop...."

Her face suddenly looked old and hard. "What's the paper about?" I asked, my voice thick from the dope shot.

"You're to act out your real-life role on film—for two thousand. Best I could get. Sign, Touie, I have a thousand things to—"

I signed, asking, "Am I still on salary, on the case?"

"Certainly." She pointed to a box in one corner of the drab detective squad room. "I brought you a suit and shirt from wardrobe—biggest I could find. Put your torn clothes down on your expense sheet."

"Thanks. Jeez, my shoes are still out on that fire escape. My wallet must be around someplace. I'll cab home and—"

"Yes, yes. Be at my office tomorrow—today—at two sharp. Now I have to get back on my horse....Oh, you have no idea *how* big this will be."

The other thing I remember was a beefy cop with captain's gold bars on his shoulders, a hard-featured face and eyes that said they hated my brown skin, telling me, "Don't think you were such a hot-shot detective, Moore. The papers will make you a hero and you'll be big time on Lenox Avenue, but we knew all about you, boy."

"You mean you knew I was down in Bingston?" The "man" was talking; I was "boy" again.

"We didn't bother looking. A wino down the hall heard this stiff argument in Thomas' room, saw a white man leaving. His wine put him to sleep but in the morning he told us. We weren't looking for you—for murder. I ain't doing anything about you kneeing that beat cop....But I'll give you some free advice: don't ever get into trouble, not even a traffic ticket. Because I ain't doing anything about you kicking a cop doesn't mean we're forgetting it."

"What was I supposed to do, let him bust my head open?" I asked, but the captain had walked away.

As it turned light outside, Ted, who had been smiling and handing out his cards as if he'd been elected mayor, told me, "Come on, Toussaint, I'll drive you home."

I finally got my wallet and stuff, and outside as I got into his car I said, "Let's get coffee. I'm empty-hungry."

"You haven't any shoes on."

"I don't drink with my shoes," I mumbled, full of tiredness.

Ted actually doubled up with stupid laughter.

TOMORROW

10

We stopped in a cafeteria on Eighty-sixth Street that was jumping with sleepy people drinking a fast cup of coffee before taking off for work. My stockinged feet didn't attract any attention, although the suit Kay got me should have been a crowd-stopper—it was made of a dark blue stiff material that simply hung on me. It was either a gag suit or custom made for a giant. The shot the doc had given me was wearing off, I was starting to feel pain, and very tired.

Ted was just the opposite. Although his eyes were bloodshot with strain and the bags under them dark as storm clouds, he was full of pep and on a talking jag. He was going to be in on the re-enacting of the McDonald capture, of course, and he kept chattering about what a break this was for his agency. After a couple of hot buttered bagels washed down with several glasses of orange juice and milk, I felt better; maybe the liquids were already replacing the blood I'd lost. But I was still blue and beat.

Ted dashed out and got the morning papers. I was all over the front page of most of them, even a small column in the *Times*. The *News* had a full-page picture of me standing in Steve's apartment, the busted window in the background. I looked out of this world—my clothes ripped and hanging in places, blood all over them and my shirt. My eyes seemed glassy, perhaps from the belt Steve gave me on the chin. Crazy the way a slim guy could punch like that. There were more pictures inside; of Kay, of Steve being led up the police-station steps, and one of Ted pointing to the recorder in the back of his car. Ted even had his coat open, showing his shoulder holster. I tried reading a few paragraphs and lost interest.

Ted read everything in a hoarse whisper, grunting with joy whenever his name was mentioned. He said, "I'm going to buy a couple dozen papers. This is worth a thousand bucks in advertising to me."

"You couldn't buy it for ten times a grand. Tell me, Ted, are you going to stop wearing two-pants suits now?"

"What's wrong with this suit? Needs pressing but—"

"Nothing. It's a beautiful hunk of cloth. Let's blow. I need my beauty rest before facing the cameras. What do you know, suddenly I'm an actor."

"Listen, Toussaint, we got some business talking to do."

"I'm exhausted. Let's chatter while you drive me home." I was too tired to be surprised at Ted's trying to hold me up for a day's pay, or whatever he wanted.

As we headed uptown, Ted chewing on a fresh cigar, he said, "I been thinking hard these last hours. You—we—have a good thing in these Madison Avenue buffs, a salting-money* deal if we act smart and fast. Remember me telling you about this industrial stuff I'm going after? TV is an industry too, a big one. They must need private dicks on a thousand deals: spying on other networks, hush up scandals, keep track of a star's drinking, protect him—or her—from babes and con men— plenty of work. By acting smart I mean this: you have the 'in'

---

* "Salting money away" means setting aside savings.

and I have the outfit. I'm offering you a partnership. Bailey and Moore. You get forty per cent. How's that, Toussaint?"

I shook my head. My eyes half closed with sleep, I was watching a TV show. Once more I was seeing Steve's apartment framed by the window, all the cockeyed furniture. Steve was "explaining" again why he killed Thomas. Kay was sitting there, calmly listening to him…agreeing with him. Cockeyed furniture, cockeyed sick people. Both of them talking like…

"I'm not chiseling you. I'd give you a straight fifty per cent only I am bringing in the equipment, a going agency, so seems to me I—"

I opened my eyes. "You can have it all, a hundred per cent, Ted. I'm throwing away my badge. I'll plug you to Kay. You'll be a cinch, the life of her parties."

We were stopped for a light. Ted turned to stare at me, the strong cigar almost in my face. "Toussaint, you know what your mouth is saying?"

"They'll be making fun of you at the parties, but it means a big buck. Actually, it isn't too hard to take or—"

"After years of starving in this racket, *now* you're giving it up?"

"Aha. Now. When for the first time I feel I know my stuff, would make a good investigator. Also give you Sid's weekend jobs too. Only time I want to hear about cops and detectives is in a novel or a movie, and maybe not even then. I've had it. Before I go to the studio today, I'm stopping at G.P.O. to tell Uncle I'm one of his new mail carriers."

"Toussaint, I figure we can't do less than ten thousand a year each, as a starter. You're wrong if you think you can go it alone or—You have something else working for you? Say, you ain't taking this acting stuff seriously?"

"Ted, I'm sick of phonies. I want to be a mailman and mind my own business. Let somebody else be waiting to collar a babe shoplifting because she hasn't money to buy the clothes she needs. I don't ever want to dun an old woman into paying up on some goddamn sink on which she was screwed from the go. Most of all I'm sick of being around people busy stepping on each other's backs, turning in their own relatives for a job, murdering them to keep the job," I said, seeing Kay again listening to Steve as if what he was telling her was normal, understandable; as if any job was worth what he did. "In short, I'm sick to death of playing in other people's dirt."

"You lost blood, you're excited, tired. Tomorrow you'll think differently about—"

"No, Ted. Maybe this has been in the back of my noggin for a long time, without me knowing it. I'm finished as a dick. You did a lot for me, Ted, and I appreciate the chance you took. I mean that. But you don't need me for this Madison Avenue rat race. I'll talk to Kay, you'll be in solid."

"If you do that, Toussaint, I'll never forget you. I'll take care of you at Christmas. I'll...you are going through with this acting business, ain't you?"

"Sure. I'll need the money to get straight. But that's it, the end of my being a badge. I'm tired. There was a farm outside Bingston. I'd like to just sit around that for a week, resting. No, no, that would drive me nuts. My stop is somewhere in the middle of the line."

"You sure need sleep."

We pulled up in front of the house—I hadn't seen the old dump in almost a week. It still looked like a dump, but such a friendly one. It really looked like home. Getting out of the car I shook Ted's hand, told him, "Thanks again. I hope this pays off big for you. Ask Kay for a good publicity man, get as much out of this hoopla as you can."

"Hey, that's good. A publicity man—sure—easily worth a couple hundred to me. Kay will show me the ropes....Suppose she won't be in her office till noon or so."

"Strike while you're hot. She's working there right now; phone her. See you this afternoon, Ted."

The apartment looked the same, as shabby and comfortable as ever. Neither Roy nor Ollie was in. I opened my studio bed, undressed. A shower was out—my body looked like a weird crossword puzzle, the patches of white tape and bandages against my brown. I couldn't recall when I was to see the doc again, made a note to phone him. It was a few minutes after eight thirty when I set the alarm for noon, fell into bed.

As if the bed was wired for sound, the second I touched the sheets the phone rang. I placed the phone on the floor, got back in bed, and picked up the receiver. It was Sybil. "Touie, I've just seen the papers....My God!"

"Hello, Sybil honey. I was going to call you later. I'll be able to pay back your money by tonight."

"Who mentioned money? Are you all right?"

"Tired—and busy. You mentioned money the last time I called you—from Kentucky. You mentioned it a lot."

"Oh, I was angry, you mixed up in all this crazy business. I mean, I thought it was nutty."

"But now that it has turned out okay, it wasn't crazy?" I asked, wondering how I'd tell her.

"Touie, I've called in sick, thinking you'd come here. What are you doing in your place? I want to talk to you."

"I have a little talking to do, too. Look, I'm in bed and pretty beat—can you come over here?"

"You know how I feel about going to your place."

"How do you feel?"

"Come on, Touie, I've told you a hundred times."

"But you never told me why, the true-blue why. Why?"

"Touie, are you drunk?"

"Only groggy. Sybil, it's important you tell me why."

"Really, you know how it looks. I mean I don't want Roy or Ollie to think I'm…You know."

"They aren't here. Yeah, I know, but what I know isn't what you know," I said, wondering if I was afraid to say what I was thinking. "Honey, if I take the P.O. job today, would you marry me and move in here?"

"Touie, what's got into you? Why on earth should we live there?"

"Sybil, I'm saying this a little mixed up, but…Babes, we have different standards, always have had, I guess. You want to marry me not because I'm *me* but because I've suddenly become a double income, a new apartment, a new car—the Harlem social swindle, which is even sillier than the Park Avenue monkey cage. You've been holding out.…"

"Touie, I don't know what you're saying. You sleep and then come over this afternoon and we'll talk."

"I have to work this afternoon and soon as I finish that I'm leaving for Ohio to pick up my car. Let's talk now, while I can say it. I don't want to talk about love like a schoolboy, but well… Maybe I can say it this way: you wouldn't marry me before because you were afraid you'd have to support me for a while. But I wasn't sitting around on my lazy rusty-dusty, I was trying to establish myself. But you wanted to hold out for a sure thing. I'm not saying this very clearly."

"You certainly aren't! I don't know what's wrong with you, Touie. As for supporting a man, I did that once and—"

"That's what I'm trying to say: I'm not talking about *a* man, or a situation, I'm talking about you and me."

"Whatever you're trying to say is over my head. Here I lose a day's pay to wait around for you and you don't come here and when I call you, you give me a lot of silly stuff!"

"It isn't silly. I've been thinking about this the last couple of days. The high point of a marriage can't be a new apartment or a fur coat or—"

"Have you turned sappy? All this talk about l-o-v-e. What's wrong with you?"

What was wrong was I didn't have the guts to tell her the truth. I tried to think of the right words and all I could think of was a line from a song: you always hurt the one you love....* But I didn't love Sybil and she never loved me. Then I kept thinking of what she'd said about when a man can't find himself he found her. That was true. I had found myself, didn't...

"Touie? Did you hear me?"

"Yeah, I heard you. Look, I can't say what I want. I'll... eh...I'll send you a check tonight."

"Just be sure you do! When you come to your senses, when you come back from Ohio, perhaps I'll let you call me and we'll talk about this when you've calmed down."

"Sybil, I want us to be friends—always—but I don't know if we'll ever talk about this...."

"All this publicity has gone to your head. Send me my money and good-by!"

She hung up and I put the phone down and stretched out in bed. I knew how it would sound: I was giving her the brush now that I had it made. But how could I tell her I didn't have it made money-wise, as Kay would say, but in my mind? In my peace of mind?

---

* "You Always Hurt the One You Love" is a song by Allan Roberts and Doris Fisher, first recorded by the Mills Brothers in 1944.

I was too tired to think about it. I felt lousy—but not too lousy. I'd been trying to tell her what I'd known for the last six or seven hours...When I drove the Jag back from Bingston I wouldn't be driving alone...I hoped.

READING GROUP GUIDE

1. Do you think that Lacy accurately captures the experience of Black men (and women) in the 1950s?

2. What do you think of Lacy's treatment of LGBT characters in the book?

3. How do you feel about the fact that Lacy took on these subjects despite being White and straight?

4. How does Touie Moore compare in your mind to other private detectives of the time (for example, Sam Spade, Philip Marlowe, Ellery Queen, or Nero Wolfe and Archie Goodwin)?

5. How did you react to Touie's decision to give up detective work?

6. Were you surprised that Touie walked away from his girlfriend, Sybil, to try to begin another relationship with Frances?

7. Are you interested enough in Touie Moore to want to read more stories in which he features?

FURTHER READING

BY LEN ZINBERG*

As Zinberg

Walk Hard—Talk Loud. Indianapolis: Bobbs-Merrill, 1940, hc.
What D'Ya Know for Sure? New York: Doubleday, 1947, hc.
Hold with the Hares. New York: Doubleday, 1948, hc.

As Ed Lacy

The Woman Aroused. New York: Avon, 1951, pb.
Sin in Their Blood. New York: Eton Books, 1952, pb.
Strip for Violence. New York: Eton Books, 1953, pb.
Enter without Desire. New York: Avon, 1954, pb.
Go for the Body. New York: Avon, 1954, pb.
The Best That Ever Did It. New York: Harper, 1955, hc.
The Men from the Boys. New York: Harper, 1956, hc.

---

* Some titles were altered in later paperback editions. Those marked "hc" are hardcover originals, and those marked "pb" are paperback originals. That is, those titles did not appear first in hardcover.

Lead with Your Left. New York: Harper, 1957, hc.
Be Careful How You Live. London: Boardman, 1958, hc.
Breathe No More, My Lady. New York: Avon, 1958, pb.
Shakedown for Murder. New York: Avon, 1958, pb.
Blonde Bait. New York: Zenith, 1959, pb.
The Big Fix. New York: Pyramid, 1960, pb.
A Deadly Affair. New York: Hillman Books, 1960, pb.
Bugged for Murder. New York: Avon, 1961, pb.
The Freeloaders. New York: Berkley, 1961, pb.
South Pacific Affair. New York: Belmont, 1961, pb.
The Sex Castle. New York: Paperback Library, 1963, pb.
Two Hot to Handle. New York: Paperback Library, 1963, pb.
Moment of Untruth. New York: Lancer, 1964, pb.
Pity the Honest. London: Boardman, 1964, pb.
Sleep in Thunder. New York: Grosset & Dunlap, 1964, hc.
Harlem Underground. New York: Pyramid, 1965, pb.
The Hotel Dwellers. New York: Harper, 1966, hc.
Double Trouble. New York: Lancer, 1967, pb.
In Black & Whitey. New York: Lancer, 1967, pb.
The Napalm Bugle. New York: Pyramid, 1968, pb.
The Big Bust. New York: Pyramid, 1969, pb.

As Steve April

Route 13. New York: Funk & Wagnalls, 1954, hc.

As Russell Turner

The Long Night. New York: Hillman Books, 1957, pb.
The Short Night. New York: Hillman Books, 1957, pb.

CRITICAL STUDIES

Bailey, Frankie Y. *Out of the Woodpile: Black Characters in Crime and Detective Fiction*. New York: Greenwood Press, 1991.

Baker, Robert A. and Michael T. Nietzel, eds. "The First Dark Knight: Toussaint Moore. Ed Lacy (Leonard S. Zinberg)." In *Private Eyes: One Hundred and One Knights—A Survey of American Detective Fiction, 1922–1984*, 102–04. Bowling Green, OH: Bowling Green State University Popular Press, 1985.

Browne, Roy B. "Ed Lacy: Passage through Darkness." In *Heroes and Humanities: Detective Fiction and Culture*, 47–54. Bowling Green, OH: Bowling Green State University Popular Press, 1986.

Hynes, Jennifer. "Ed Lacy (Len Zinberg) (1911–7 January 1968)," *Dictionary of Literary Biography*, vol. 226, *American Hard-Boiled Crime Writers*, edited by George Parker Anderson and Julie B. Anderson, 226–32. Detroit: Gale Group, 2000.

Lachman, Marv. "Ed Lacy: Paperback Writer of the Left." In *Murder Off the Rack: Critical Studies of Ten Paperback Masters*, edited by Jon L. Breen and Martin H. Greenberg, 15–34. Metuchen, NJ: Scarecrow Press, 1989.

Lynskey, Ed. "Ed Lacy: New York City Crime Author." *Mystery File* 45, August 2004. http://www.mysteryfile.com/Lacy/Profile.html.

Muller, Marcia and Bill Pronzini, eds. *1001 Midnights: The Aficionado's Guide to Mystery and Detective Fiction*. New York: Arbor House, 1986.

Robinson, Vicki K. "Ed Lacy/Leonard S. Zinberg." In *Critical Survey of Mystery and Detective Fiction*, vol. 3, edited by Frank N. Magill, 1017–20. Pasadena, CA: Salem Press, 1988.

Woods, Paula L. *Spooks, Spies & Private Eyes: Black Mystery, Crime, and Suspense Fiction of the 20th Century*. New York: Bantam Doubleday Dell, 1995.

ABOUT THE AUTHOR

Leonard "Len" S. Zinberg (1911–1968) is a name virtually unknown today, even among crime fiction aficionados. Born in New York (probably New York City) to Max and Elizabeth Zinberg, he lived in Manhattan after his father's death and his mother's remarriage in 1921. His stepfather, Maxwell "Mac" Wycoff, was a banking lawyer with a large firm, and they lived the affluent lives of White professionals on 153rd Street, near Harlem. During the 1920s and 1930s, Zinberg attended the College of the City of New York and traveled throughout the United States, working odd jobs. By the 1940s, he had returned to New York City, where he married Esther Flatts, a Black woman; had a daughter, Carla; and began supporting his family as a freelance writer.

Zinberg's first writing appeared under his own name in various magazines and literary journals in the form of short stories and essays. His first novel appeared in 1940, titled *Walk Hard—Talk Loud*, and combined his love of boxing with a thoughtful examination of race relations. The back cover of the paperback edition summed up the book:

Boxing racketeers, loose-hipped blondes, chiselers—these were all part of Andy Whitman's life—and so were jim-crow hotels, cops, tenements, and hatred. For Andy Whitman was a Negro trying to make a living in the toughest racket in the world, the prize ring. Tried to make a living—until the crooks and the vultures moved in. [*]

Ralph Ellison, in a review titled "Negro Prize Fighter" for *New Masses*, praised the book for "indicat[ing] how far a writer, whose approach to Negro life is uncolored by condescension, stereotyped ideas, and other faults growing out of race prejudice, is able to go with a Marxist understanding of the economic basis of Negro personality."[†] Such praise, and Zinberg's friendships in the Black community, gave a real boost to the novel. Adapted for the stage by Zinberg with the Black producer Abram Hills, this was Zinberg's first taste of real success. However, he likely had mixed feelings when the play was moved to Broadway and Mickey "the Toy Bulldog" Walker, the middleweight champion, was cast in the lead—Walker was White.

World War II interrupted Zinberg's life in New York, sending him to Italy. There, he continued to write, with stories and war sketches appearing in many venues. When he returned home, he contributed eighteen pieces to the *New Yorker* magazine between 1945 and 1947. Zinberg continued to write novels as well because, he learned, they paid better than the

---

[*] Len Zinberg, *Walk Hard—Talk Loud* (New York: Lion Books, 1950).

[†] Ralph Ellison, "Negro Prize Fighter," *New Masses* 37, no. 13 (December 17, 1940): 26–27. Ellison, the eminent Black intellectual, knew Zinberg was White, but others were confused about the race of "Ed Lacy." One of his earliest short stories, "The Right Thing," was first printed in the Baltimore newspaper *Afro-American* and later in a collection from that publication, Nick Aaron Ford and H. L. Faggett, eds., *Best Short Stories by Afro-American Writers* (Boston: Meador, 1950). Lacy is also listed in Theressa Gunnels Rush, ed., *Black American Writers, Past and Present: A Biographical and Bibliographical Dictionary* (Metuchen, NJ: Scarecrow Press, 1975).

stories he sold to the pulp magazines. Hardcover novels were soon to be eclipsed in sales, however, by paperback originals.* Zinberg leaped into that market, using the pen name of "Ed Lacy."† His first three novels—*The Woman Aroused* (1951), *Sin in Their Blood* (1952), and *Strip for Violence* (1953)—had typically lurid titles and garish, sexy cover art but were well written and tightly plotted. He returned to hardcover for his next two Lacy novels, *The Best That Ever Did It* (1955) and *The Men from the Boys* (1956), working with the prestigious editor Joan Kahn at Harper.

Lacy's crowning achievement was the publication in 1957 of *Room to Swing*, featuring private investigator Toussaint Moore, which won the Edgar Award of the Mystery Writers of America for Best Mystery Novel.‡ Critic Ed Gorman wrote:

There was a lyricism, almost a poetry, to the writing that touched not only the powerful, melancholy storyline but also the elegant and evocative place descriptions. I've always regarded this as a true masterpiece. Certainly its take on

---

* Modern paperbacks were introduced in 1935 by Penguin in England as cheap and portable reprints of its hardcover novels, though in fact many books were originally published in softcover format as early as 1900. They soon spread to the United States and were widely sold to soldiers as well as those who stayed home during World War II. By 1950, American publishers began to commission original fiction for their paperback lines.

† The origin of Zinberg's pen name is unknown, but critics have speculated that Zinberg wanted to separate the crime writer from his political liberalism (expressed in books like his *Hold with the Hares* [New York: Doubleday, 1948], about 1930s leftist politics) and interest in the Communist Party. This was, after all, the era of McCarthyism and the blacklisting of writers. See "Ed Lacy: New York City Crime Author" by Ed Lynskey, *Mystery File* 45 (August 2004), http://www.mysteryfile.com /Lacy/Profile.html, and Alan Wald's entry on Zinberg in Mary Jo Buhle, Paul Buhle, and Dan Georgakas, eds., *Encyclopedia of the American Left* (New York: Oxford University Press, 1998).

---

‡ The Edgar for the "Best Paperback Original" was not presented until 1970.

race makes it a milestone too...I liked several other Lacy novels very much, too, but Room [to Swing] is the one that got him to heaven.[*]

Several other scholars also have placed the book on their lists of favorites.[†]

It took seven years for Zinberg to pen another mystery about Toussaint Moore, the paperback original *Moment of Untruth* (1964). It again explores the Black experience, this time outside the United States, in Mexico, where Moore finds himself stereotyped as a bruiser and a sexual predator and mistaken for another Black man. At the same time, Moore recognizes a certain freedom in a society in which persons of his color are not all stigmatized and discovers that there are even lower castes than Black people in some parts of the world.

Zinberg created other Black heroes, especially police detective Lee Hayes, who appears in *Harlem Underground* (1965) and *In Black & Whitey* (1967). These novels bring Hayes into discussions of racial inequality in America, where Zinberg, through Hayes, expresses the value of interracial compassion in society. This compassion may be seen in earlier novels as well, such as *The Woman Aroused* (1951), Lacy's first hard-boiled fiction, in which a leftist character who kills a Puerto Rican hit man is troubled by issues of class and privilege, and *Sin in Their Blood* (1952), in which Blacks who pass as White are blackmailed, while the White police treat a sympathetic Black housekeeper with scorn.

---

* Quoted in Lynskey, "Ed Lacy."

---

† The revered mystery critic Anthony Boucher listed the novel among the best of 1957; Marv Lachman included it on his list of the "important" books between 1950 and 1969 and again on his list of 150 favorite novels from 1913 to 2001; and Gary Warren Niebuhr included it in his "One Hundred Classics and Highly Recommended Titles." (All of these lists may be found in Roger M. Sobin, ed., *The Essential Mystery Lists: For Readers, Collectors, and Librarians* [Phoenix: Poisoned Pen Press, 2007].)

Zinberg had a lot to say about writers and writing and he seemed to have a clear-eyed view of himself, expressed mainly in an article called "I Dunit" for *P.S.* magazine in August 1966[*]:

> [*Unlike my characters,*] *I'm a most gentle fellow, the kind-to-animals type, who hasn't been in a fist fight since school days, nor have I ever been arrested—not even a traffic ticket. I've never known a real thug, although I know some petty hustlers. I can't solve a real crime, haven't been a cop and I'm a pathetic four beer drunk... I'm a full time, working, freelance writer, and if you want to call me a hack, I won't be terribly upset. Every person who makes his pork chops from the sale of words is a hack, whether he realizes it or not. I also believe all fiction writers, including us honest hacks, are creative writers. You'd be astonished at the creative drive and skill needed to turn out formula stories.*

He went on to discuss his subject matter:

> *The creative writer, with his deep curiosity about his fellow beings, must care about people, which is rapidly becoming a rare trait in our cynical world. I have never written anything I considered anti-human, jingoistic or bigoted. True, my stories often deal with violence and sex, but neither were invented by writers. (Although there are attempts to shoulder blame on us!) You'll find more real violence and brutality in the daily headlines than any fiction writer could dream up. We live in an age where the screams of a girl being stabbed to death aroused a*

[*] Reprinted on *The New Thrilling Detective Website*, March 21, 2019, https:// thrillingdetective.com/2019/03/31/i-dunit/.

dozen or so average citizens, sitting in their homes, and not one even bothered to call the police, where Civil Rights workers are murdered and the killers rarely brought to trial or found guilty.[*]

At the time he wrote this insightful piece, he was promoting his latest attempt at commercial success, a hardcover mainstream novel called *The Hotel Dwellers.*[†] He had high hopes that this might lead to another "straight" novel, but sadly, the book did not sell well, and Zinberg died of a heart attack on January 7, 1968. Two more paperback originals were published posthumously, *The Napalm Bugle* (1968) and *The Big Bust* (1969), both under his "Lacy" byline. Thirty-five novels of Zinberg's, all but six of them as Lacy, were published, selling millions of copies. The *New York Times*'s obituary of Zinberg[‡] credited him with "hundreds" of short stories, but to date, no one has published a definitive bibliography of his work.[§]

---

[*] Zinberg refers to the Kitty Genovese case in Queens and the three "Freedom Summer" murders that occurred in Mississippi, all in 1964.

[†] Published by Harper & Row under the "Ed Lacy" name. Harper mistakenly billed it as a "Harper Novel of Suspense," inserting into some copies a disclaimer that admitted the error and terming the book an "adult novel."

[‡] "Leonard Zinberg, Wrote as Ed Lacy," *New York Times* (January 8, 1968), 35.

[§] The most complete bibliography can be found in Jennifer Hynes, "Ed Lacy (Len Zinberg) (1911–7 January 1968)," *Dictionary of Literary Biography*, vol. 226, *American Hard-Boiled Crime Writers*, edited by George Parker Anderson and Julie B. Anderson (Detroit: Gale Group, 2000), 226–32.